First Class
ROMANCE

First Class
ROMANCE

CAMILLE HOPE

GREATER INK

Los Angeles

Greater
Ink
greaterink.com

ISBN 979-8-9907066-0-6 (paperback)
ISBN 979-8-9907066-1-3 (ebook)

Library of Congress Control Number: 2024941211

Classification: Romance Fiction, Novels

Book design by Greater Ink
Cover illustration by Kate Hamernik

Printed in the United States of America

For my grandmother, Maxine.

1

Emy

EMERSON NICHOLS WAS ON THE GO AGAIN. At almost thirty-three, she was single, living alone in a charming West Village apartment in Manhattan, and waiting for her next adventure. It was December 23, and she had nowhere to be for the holidays.

Emy had intentionally swapped a shift with a coworker so they could be home with their family for Christmas. She had done the same for New Year's Eve, allowing a friend to hang out in Times Square to watch the ball drop. Emy knew nothing about having a family, and the only ringing she'd hear on New Year's Eve would be her alarm clock.

"Yes, Marie. I'm leaving you again. But don't worry, sweet girl, I'll be back in a few days." Marie, her beautiful white fluffy Persian cat, was curled up in Emy's open suitcase. She was very familiar with Emy's comings and goings.

Thankfully, Emy had great neighbor kids who loved Marie just as much as Emy did. Possibly more. They knew her schedule each month and had a key to the apartment. Marie wasn't getting any younger and loved her apartment life. Having the kids next door gave Emy peace of mind knowing Marie was being loved and cared for.

"C'mon, you. I've got packing to do, and I don't want to be covered in cat hair on this trip." Emy picked up the fur ball and deposited her on the window seat of her Manhattan apartment. With a big stretch and soft purr, Marie found the one sunny spot and promptly returned to sleep.

Emy was a pro at packing her bag. She had been a flight attendant for Infinite Airlines since she was twenty-one. Emy's life was one of adventure, filled with stories of the places she had visited and the people she had met. Her career had provided experiences others could only dream about. Her journey as a flight attendant broadened her horizons and allowed her to explore the world in a more abundant way that few others could match.

However, not everything had gone as she had planned. She would be alone again on another holiday.

Stop that, Emy. Let's not feel sorry for ourselves tonight. We're going to be in Paris on Christmas morning.

Trying to focus on the positive, she reminded herself she had swapped to work a flight from New York to Paris, a destination that held a touch of magic during the holiday season. With her seniority at Infinite, Emy was now able to pick and choose her destinations. Some of her coworkers were not so lucky.

She turned her attention to her suitcase, which lay open on her bed. Carefully, she folded her clothes, knowing that she must pack efficiently for this overnight flight. The prospect of spending Christmas Day in the beautiful city of Paris filled her with joy and a hint of longing.

Emy's phone chimed, signaling a new message from her best friend and fellow flight attendant, Chloe.

CHLOE Ready for a trip down the Champs-Élysées? Paris, here we come!

With a huge smile, Emy fired back…

EMY Are you kidding me? Did you really get on this trip with me? This might be the best Christmas gift ever, Chloe.

Emy's eyes filled with tears. She loved that her friend had managed to join her on the flight. She had been hoping but hadn't heard yet.

CHLOE Oui, madame! And we are going to make this the most memorable Christmas flight ever.

Emy might not be with her immediate family on Christmas Day. But she would have Chloe, which was more than enough.

Chloe was her partner in crime. They became fast friends during flight attendant training and had been best friends and roommates ever since. They tried to sync flight schedules together as much as possible. Chloe had recently moved out of their shared apartment and moved into her fiancé's townhouse. Even though they were just a few blocks apart, it felt like Chloe had moved to another city.

Emy was thrilled for Chloe. It would be hard to see her go if Patrick weren't such a catch. But she was happy her friend had finally found love. Even if it meant Emy was alone a lot of the time now. She was excited to be flying with her in the morning. With both of them speaking fairly fluent French, it was easy to get scheduled together on flights to and from Europe.

As she zipped up her suitcase and placed it by the front door, she couldn't help but feel a rush of anticipation and another feeling she wasn't entirely sure of. There was something magical about flying on Christmas Eve, sharing this time with her friend as they crossed the Atlantic. And after all, it was Paris, with its sparkling lights, charming streets, and delicious food. It would be the perfect place to celebrate the holiday.

Emy was ready to go to bed. She wanted to get a good night's sleep so she'd be ready to start her Christmas adventure in the skies. She completed a final sweep of her apartment, ensuring everything was tidy before leaving.

Before she clicked off the last of the lights, she checked her uniform, slid her fingers over the gold wing pin that spelled out her name, and proudly displayed the Infinite Airlines logo—just like her mother had many years before her. Even though part of her wished she wasn't so alone at times, she was exactly where she was meant to be.

∞

BEEP, BEEP, BEEP, BEEP, BEEP, BEEP… NO MATTER HOW OFTEN EMY HEARD HER ALARM GOING OFF, SHE WAS NEVER READY TO GET UP. It would take several hits of the snooze button before she could drag herself out of bed. Today, she had lost track of how many snooze button hits she needed to finally wake up. Grateful she had packed the night before, she headed into the kitchen where her coffee machine was waiting.

As her coffee brewed, Marie circled her feet below, letting out a tiny cry, signaling she was hungry.

"C'mon girl, let's get you taken care of."

Walking over to the other side of her tiny kitchen, she grabbed Marie's bowl and filled it with her favorite dry food. Emy sat at the kitchen table to sip her coffee and watch Marie eat breakfast. Reaching down, she rubbed the cat between her ears.

"Glad one of us likes to eat first thing in the morning."

Emy got up and rinsed out her mug before heading into the bathroom to get ready for her trip.

After a quick shower, she opted for one more cup of coffee before she was ready to head out. She would finish getting ready in the crew lounge once she arrived at the airport. She needed to allow three and a half hours if she wanted to be at JFK on time for her shift. The hour it took to commute was long, but living in the West Village was worth it. When Emy's parents retired, they decided to let Emy stay in their apartment rent-free. There was no way she could ever afford a place in the West Village otherwise.

Dragging her rollerboard suitcase down the stairs, she had a ten-minute walk ahead of her through Greenwich Village to catch the A train. She allowed enough time to pick Chloe up along the way so they could ride in together. She was almost to Chloe's when she typed out a quick message...

EMY Two minutes away, meet me out front?

Emy was glad for the hour-long commute ahead so the two could catch up. It was strange not living with Chloe anymore, and she couldn't wait to hear how shacking up with Patrick was going.

"Ohmygawd. Can it be any colder? We need to hurry!"

Chloe stood on the stoop of her brownstone, shifting from side to side to stay warm. She clumsily pulled her roller bag down the steps to join Emy on the sidewalk.

Emy rolled her eyes. "Yes, yes, it can be colder, so don't put that out into the world, or it will happen. Let's go, let's go!"

The two began walking briskly, pulling their bags behind them. It was just hovering around freezing, and the skies seemed to threaten snow. They needed to get to the train before that happened.

Rounding the corner, they made it to the subway cold but dry. They boarded the train and settled into the commute. As the train made its way along the tracks, Emy and Chloe found themselves engrossed in a heartfelt conversation about Chloe's upcoming wedding. They had spent countless hours in the air together, serving passengers with smiles and professionalism. But now, during this rare break, they had a chance to delve into more personal matters. Living apart for the last few months, Emy realized how much she missed her friend.

"Okay, Emy, talk to me. You seem down."

Chloe was usually the needy one, with Emy reassuring her. But over the last few weeks, it was obvious that something was off with Emy.

Emy glanced around the train. Everywhere she looked, there was a couple sitting cozily together. She wished she had a companion she could hold hands with, someone to laugh at her jokes, or someone to travel with her. Emy had great flight perks, and she'd love to be able to share them with someone special.

Watching the couple across from her made her chest tight. The last thing she wanted to do was share these feelings with Chloe. They had these conversations before. But that was when Chloe was still single and living with her. Emy wasn't naive. She knew this day would come. But if anyone told her Chloe would be getting married before her, she would have said that was crazy.

"I don't know, it's nothing. I'm sure it's just being alone during the holidays that has me feeling sorry for myself. It's strange not having someone to watch *Friends* with every night before bed."

Both girls sat in silence. It had been their nightly tradition to fall asleep on the couch watching their favorite TV show until one of them woke up and coaxed the other to go to bed too. Chloe leaned in to remind Emy that she knew how to turn the TV off on her own. Even before they were roommates, Emy had managed without her.

"I know, it's strange. For the first time, I know what it's like to be alone. I'm not sure I like it anymore." Emy stared out the window, watching the passing train.

"You could always get another roommate," Chloe said flatly. "But, you know I am not replaceable."

"No. No way. I am officially too old for a roommate. Besides, who could replace you?"

Emy leaned in and rested her head on Chloe's shoulder. The two had become more like sisters over the years. With no brothers and sisters of her own, and with her parents on the go, Chloe was her only family.

"Well, that was the nicest thing anyone has said to me today."

Chloe offered a sarcastic grin just in time to realize they had arrived at JFK airport.

∞

THE RIDE INTO JFK HAD LEFT EMY THINKING ABOUT HER APARTMENT AND IF SHE SHOULD FIND A NEW ROOMMATE AFTER ALL. It just seemed so daunting, and people were crazy. Living with Chloe all these years seemed to set her up for failure if she looked for anyone else. Not everyone would leave their fiancé at Christmas to be with their friend. Emy and Chloe both knew this was the last holiday they'd spend together as single women. Patrick, God bless him, wanted the girls to have one last Christmas together and encouraged Chloe to make it happen.

Walking into the airport terminal, Emy and Chloe headed to the crew lounge to check in for their trip. After a quick crew briefing, the girls walked fast and briskly to the airplane. They would still need to do preflight safety checks before they could board the passengers.

"Before we meet 300 of our closest friends, do you want me to grab anything from the book shop?" Chloe asked before splitting off from Emy and heading into the bookstore.

"No, I'm good. I'll meet you on the plane."

Emy looked at her crew sheet one more time to double check her gate number. She casually walked through the terminal, noticing the many passengers sitting in the gate areas and wondering where they were headed. So many people had places to go, she thought.

She had just talked to her parents the night before, wishing them a Merry Christmas. They were spending the holiday in Bali. After working many Christmas holidays themselves, they always found themselves in a warm weather destination that lacked tourists during the holiday weeks. They'd be back through New York at some point after the New Year.

With the flash of her badge and a quick verification from the gate agent, Emy pulled her bags down the jet bridge to the airplane. With her impressive French skills, she'd be working first class going over to Paris.

Unfortunately, that also meant Chloe would be back in economy, as two French speakers in the same cabin rarely happened. Emy stowed her bag in an overhead bin in the economy cabin and walked up the aisle to the front of the plane. She started to prepare the cabin along with her other colleagues, Jeff and Allen. Any minute now, they'd start boarding.

2

Jackson

JACKSON RILEY SAT IN DISBELIEF AT HIS LUCK IN THE AIRPORT LOUNGE, WAITING FOR HIS FLIGHT TO PARIS ON CHRISTMAS EVE. He was the youngest at the family gallery, and he was also single. Everyone else in the family had commitments. So it made sense for him to go. Having a first-class seat almost took the sting out of being on a long-haul flight on Christmas Eve.

With no return ticket yet confirmed, he couldn't help but feel a little agitated. As much as he loved Paris, he didn't want to be gone too long. Taking the final drink from his glass, he set his glass down and made his way to the gate.

As he approached his gate, he was just coming to terms with the trip, but then he heard the boarding call and everything changed.

"Ladies and gentlemen, at this time, we'd like to invite members of our first-class cabin to begin the boarding process for Flight 222 to Paris, Charles de Gaulle. We kindly ask that our business-class passengers and any passengers requiring additional assistance make their way to the gate agents for priority boarding at this time."

Well, no turning back now. Christmas in Paris it is. Alone. Jackson stood up straight and collected himself before walking down the jet bridge, noting he'd be spending the next seven hours by himself.

Normally he wouldn't mind the trip. He knew being single would eventually catch up to him. Apparently, today was the day. There was nothing he could do about it now. He hadn't dated seriously in months. He also wasn't going to rush into a relationship just to get more seniority in the family lineup during the holidays.

Jackson knew what he was missing. He had spent the last few years watching his sisters expand their families. As much as he loved being the "cool" uncle, he was starting to wonder if a family of his own would happen.

As he made the trek down the jetway, he had a lot to think about. For now, he just wanted to get to Paris as quickly as possible so he could get his job done and return home in time for the New Year.

Just as he approached the boarding door, he felt a buzz in his pocket. He pulled out his phone and saw a text from his sister Jessica.

JESSICA Sorry you drew the short end of the stick. If we
didn't have that event next week, you know I would
have gone in your place.

He knew Jessica genuinely felt bad for him. But the last thing he wanted was for her to feel guilty and not enjoy her holidays.

JACKSON Don't worry about it, but you'll miss me
tomorrow morning. Mark my words!

He sighed. It was his turn to board. He flicked open the boarding pass on his phone and stepped over the threshold and onto the airplane. Jackson really did like to travel, but the timing couldn't have been worse.

Emy

EMY WAS POSITIONED AT THE BOARDING DOOR GREETING EAGER, CHEERFUL PASSENGERS WHEN SHE NOTICED A GUY COMING DOWN THE JET BRIDGE. She thought momentarily that he would be really hot if he didn't look so grumpy. With his arms full, he managed to flash his phone her way, revealing his name and seat number. Great. He'd be up front with her in first class.

"Ah. Good evening, Mr. Riley. Welcome aboard Infinite Airlines. We're delighted to have you in our first-class cabin this evening. It looks like you're in seat 1A. Please let us know if we can do anything to make your flight as comfortable and enjoyable as possible."

Why is he looking at me like he's about to bite me? She moved aside and motioned for him to make his way to his seat.

Working first class might have its perks, but there were times when the folks seated in economy were more approachable. She had been thinking this when she noticed Mr. Riley still standing in the entryway.

"I'm sorry. Did you need something, sir?" Emy waited patiently for his response, but instead, she heard a grumble as he finally walked away.

Emy could see Chloe making her way forward to begin the preflight beverage service for the first-class passengers.

"Anyone we know up front tonight?" Chloe asked as she peeked past Emy's shoulder.

"No, but check out the guy in 1A. I really don't think Mr. Grumpypants is going to enjoy the next seven hours with me." Emy made a face only Chloe could see as she began to stroll the first-class aisle.

As Emy greeted each passenger coming on board, she would occasionally steal a look over her shoulder in the first-class cabin. Every seat was full, and Chloe would soon be offering champagne to those already in their seats.

Mr. Riley was finally settling in, but he seemed far from comfortable. He was pulling out devices and putting away his bag. But it was hard not to notice he seemed quite mad at someone or something. Chloe picked up a tray from the galley and started her pre-departure beverage service.

"Good evening, Mr. Riley. Would you like a glass of champagne before we take off?"

Chloe held the tray level with Mr. Riley, but kept her eyes on him while he continued to shuffle around.

"No, thank you." It was barely audible, but Chloe got the hint.

Returning to stand next to Emy, Chloe said, "Yah, good luck with 'hot guy' in 1A. Seems pretty annoyed, even before you get to tell him you're out of his first choice meal." They laughed out loud.

Emy made one final pre-departure announcement while Chloe returned to her assigned cabin.

Emy hung up the airplane phone and walked back up to the nose where the first-class galley was located. It was small. Perfect for the three flight attendants that would be working the Boeing 777 first-class cabin. Tonight, all twelve passengers would be getting the best service from Infinite's finest flight attendants.

Even Mr. Riley.

She waited for the flight deck to make their welcome announcements and the inflight crew to secure the cabin doors. Once she got the final call that all the doors were secure, Emy reached for the inflight control panel and started the safety video. She slowly walked down the aisle, checking that everything was stored safely and seat belts were buckled, then made her way back to her jumpseat for take-off.

The flight deck gave the signal they were ready to go, and Emy double-checked her shoulder harness. It wasn't until they were rolling down the runway that she noticed she had a perfect view of 1A. She was always curious about her passengers; this was no exception.

Usually, her passengers were better at hiding their feelings. Mr. Riley was not, which piqued her curiosity.

∞

THEY HAD BEEN AIRBORNE FOR TWENTY MINUTES, AND IT WAS TIME TO GET TO WORK. Emy was working first class with two other flight attendants she knew well and enjoyed working with. This would make the trip go by quickly.

"Emy! Did you see that guy in 1A?" Jeff asked.

Jeff had been flying for nearly twenty years. He made their job easy, as he knew the galley like the back of his hand. She was excited to be working with him again.

"Oh yeah, hard to miss Mr. Riley. That's who you're talking about, right? Does he need something already?"

Emy peeked around the corner as she tied on her serving apron. He didn't look like he needed anything, but Jeff had her curious. Being seated in 1A meant he was close to the galley. She knew she needed to keep her voice down so no passengers in the first row would hear their conversations.

"No, but I thought you might like to take *left* side tonight. You never know. This might be your gift from Santa."

Jeff was always trying to find "the one" for Emy. He had been with his partner for many years and loved playing matchmaker for everyone else. He would not rest until she was off the market, settled, and happy.

However, she was a catch, and he had repeatedly told her not to settle. Her future partner was out there. It would just take time to find him.

"That would mean that I was good this year, Jeff. And we both know I might have misstepped a time or two. No Christmas wishes for me this year."

Jeff gave her a pouty look.

"Sorry, I know you're disappointed." Emy made a dramatic sigh as she gave Jeff a side hug before they both got to work.

She declined his offer and chose the opposite side of the aircraft. She wasn't in the mood to figure out what was happening with 1A over on the left. Instead, her coworker Allen swept in. Allen was someone she knew well and liked working with. He had been flying long before her and had a knack for making people feel welcome, even if their vibe was off for whatever reason.

Since there were only twelve seats in first class, Emy and Allen would be offering personal service to each passenger. Emy had spent the last few minutes looking over the manifest to get to know the six passengers she'd be working with. Jeff handed Allen a tray of hot towels and tongs.

"Emy, are *we* still single?" Like Jeff, Allen always tried to set her up and encouraged her to put herself out there more. Although there was a heavy emphasis on the "we" part of that question, Allen was also very taken.

Both Jeff and Allen were a lot older than Emy. That was one of the reasons she loved working with them, especially on holidays. They both had her best interests and piled on their fatherly advice.

Taking the tray of hot towels from Jeff, she confirmed her current relationship status.

"Yep, still single, living alone, well… there's Marie. But no prospects in sight. And thanks, but no thanks on 1A. He seems to be in a bad mood, and I don't want it to impact my holiday cheer."

Plus, he was a passenger, and Emy had a strict no-passenger and no-crew dating policy. She had done both, and neither had gone well. Her parents were one of the few exceptions as far as she could tell. Inflight relationships never worked out, unless you were just looking for a hookup, which she was not.

The first-class dinner service was a well-orchestrated event, especially with a master running the galley. Jeff had everything prepped and ready to go, making each course transition seamless. It was a privilege working first class, and Emy took her position seriously, ensuring each passenger felt like a guest in a five-star restaurant.

It was important not to rush the passengers, so she spent time talking to each person, making sure their needs were met.

She tried her best not to look over at 1A, but it was hard not to, given the size of the cabin. Plus, she could hear Allen trying to engage with him. It wasn't working.

As they started closing up the galley from the night's dinner service, Allen confirmed what she already knew. 1A was easy on the eyes but had no interest in engaging with anyone.

"What did I miss?" Chloe hopped into the galley, grabbing a handful of leftover nuts and popping them in her mouth.

She had come up to replace Emy while she went on her rest break. Chloe was everyone's favorite. She was full of life and always brought the house down.

"Get the skinny on 1A yet?"

Allen walked over to join Chloe and started picking out what remained of the cashews from the bowl of nuts. "Nothing yet. The night is young. Give me some time. I'll get him to open up; I always do."

Allen walked away, but not before they caught the wink sent in Emy's direction.

"You all need to stop it. I'm not interested." She looked back and forth to Chloe and Jeff, who both knew how to irritate her. She untied her apron. "I'm going on my break."

The meal service was complete, and the galley was clean. The cabin was quiet, and most everyone would sleep for the next few hours. Including Emy.

She tossed her apron aside and headed to the back of the plane for a couple of hours of rest. As she wandered to the back, she noticed the majority of passengers were already sleeping and envied them.

Emy could never sleep on her rest breaks. Instead, she put in her AirPods and listened to her favorite playlist. For the first time in a long time, she was lonely. She hated this time on flights when she desperately wanted to sleep but couldn't because her mind was wandering.

Dating apps were not for her, so the prospect of meeting someone was slim with her travel schedule. She was gone at least three days each week, and she was pretty set with her routine. It would take someone remarkable to be willing to go with her flow. Someone who loved to travel as much as she did. Not that it was even a consideration. But 1A—Mr. Grumpypants— did not look like traveling was his thing.

Emy started thinking of ways she could put herself out there. Everything she could come up with, she had already tried. Or the thought was too depressing. The thoughts must have been exhausting because she finally dozed off.

∞

"WAKE UP, SLEEPING BEAUTY." Chloe was standing on the top steps in the crew bunk area and started crawling over to her.

The rest area was small, but it allowed the crew to have a decent place to rest on long-haul flights. However, she couldn't stand up in the narrow aisle leading back to where Emy was resting on a bunk.

"What are you thinking about?" Chloe was already removing her shoes. It was her time to get a quick rest break in.

"I was dreaming about dinner tonight. I really hope they have those desserts we had last time."

Emy sat up and glanced in the tiny mirror hooked on the wall. Then she grabbed her makeup kit to cover the bags under her eyes. No amount of makeup would help her now. She looked forward to having a few days off when they got back home. Apparently, she needed it.

∞

ONE OF EMY'S FAVORITE PARTS OF OVERNIGHT FLIGHTS WAS CATCHING THE SUNRISE. After freshening up from her rest break, she sat in the galley jumpseat, taking a moment to appreciate the sun welcoming them into another day. They had another hour and a half of flight time. One more meal service, and they'd be on the ground in Paris.

"Hey, champ. Coffee?" Jeff was already in the galley getting it set up and ready for the final meal service. This one was much easier. The smell of the freshly brewed coffee usually had passengers stirring and waking up.

"Sure. Thanks."

Emy was tying up her apron when Jeff crossed over to hand her a cup of the hot coffee. She took it and noticed the cream had already been added. He really did know her well.

"You know, we just want the best for you. I've known you for over ten years now. You really are a catch. Don't settle."

The two were quiet as they passed a few more minutes and waited for Allen to join them from his rest break.

"And whatever you do, don't listen to us. We've been married so long that we've forgotten how fabulous it is to be single. Enjoy it while you can. One day, not too far off, you'll be in our shoes, living vicariously through the next young new hire hanging out with us in the galley." Jeff was talking and plating pieces of French toast at the same time.

Leaning against the doorway with coffee in hand, Emy was about to say something when a disheveled 1A pulled back the galley curtain.

How is it possible to look so good first thing in the morning? And is he even taller now?

As he stood on the other side of the galley directly across from her, Emy suddenly felt very small. His hair was in all directions, but he still managed to look effortlessly stylish. The tousled look gave him a rugged and carefree appearance that was suddenly endearing. This disheveled look was unintentional, but that made him even more attractive. It was as if he could turn even the most casual moments into a part of his daily appeal without realizing it.

Jeff cleared his throat again to get Emy's attention. But apparently, she had been staring at Mr. Riley for some time and didn't hear Jeff talking to her.

"Emy? Ahem, Emerson? Can you help Mr. Riley with his coffee, please?" Jeff, trying hard to hide his grin, handed her a ceramic mug from the galley cart.

"Oh, excuse me, of course! Cream? Sugar?"

As she filled the cup with hot coffee, she wondered how long she had been staring at him. *What an idiot!* Even Jeff had noticed and stepped in to save her.

"Black. Black's fine. Thanks."

As she handed Mr. Riley the mug of hot coffee, their fingers briefly touched, and they exchanged a fleeting but charged moment. Their eyes met, and for a second, she thought she recognized a hint of a smile playing on his lips. It was a small yet intimate moment that left her feeling excited.

Quickly pulling away, she retreated to the other side of the galley. What was happening? Had it really been that long since she had connected with a man? She really was desperate if she thought there was a spark there. Certainly, she had imagined it. Or was it wishful thinking on her part?

"So, Mr. Riley, what brings you to Paris on Christmas Day?" Jeff asked.

Jeff was quick to read the room and could see that Emy was still standing there in a state of bewilderment while she fidgeted with the tie on her apron.

"It's Jackson. I'm not old enough yet for Mr. Riley."

Jackson shifted his weight, running a hand through his hair with one hand and holding the hot coffee mug in the other.

"Here for work. As you can imagine, everyone else at work had plans, so I took one for the team."

As though he said too much, he stopped and ended with "Merry Christmas" before abruptly returning to his seat.

However, it wasn't lost on anyone that as he was leaving, he gave a very notable nod in Emy's direction.

Jeff turned abruptly to her and mouthed, "What was that about?"

Emy shrugged. Apparently, a good night's sleep did wonders for some people. Jackson Riley was no exception. She waited until the galley curtain was closed before she let out her breath. She didn't realize she had been holding it.

As Allen walked casually back to the galley, he noticed Jackson returning to his seat. Allen entered the galley, grabbed an apron off the hook, and commanded, "Spill." He was tying his apron as he waited.

"I have no idea what you're talking about," Emy said, making herself busy, pulling orange juice cartons from the cart to fill up the glasses Jeff had set out.

Allen and Jeff both gave her a telling look.

In truth, she was still trying to figure out if she was making something out of nothing. But there was no denying there had been a spark. With just the briefest touch, Emy felt a fluttering deep in her soul. Something faint she had not felt in a long time. Regardless, nothing could possibly come of a simple spark and a nod. She reached up and touched her cheek, wondering why she was so flushed.

It was Christmas. She was always a little lonely and nostalgic. She was just missing her parents and feeling sorry for herself.

"Emy, seriously, why don't you take the left this time around?" Allen was already walking out to the right, not giving her much of a choice.

Emy would soon be in full view of Jackson for the remainder of the flight. Thankful it was only a short time, she made her way out into the aisle wearing her best smile.

4

Jackson

JACKSON HAD SPENT MOST OF THE FLIGHT LISTENING TO CHATTER BEHIND THE GALLEY CURTAIN. Apparently, this crew was tight and had been flying with one another for several years. He gleaned that the two male flight attendants thought highly of their partner… *Emy*, was it?

Listening in felt very wrong, but he had no desire to watch a movie or listen to music. Still aggravated that his family booked him a flight on Christmas Eve without any regard, he was in no mood for niceties. He would rather wallow in self-pity, and that's exactly what he did for almost four of the seven hours of the flight.

However, listening to the crew, he found it hard to believe the cute flight attendant behind the curtain had a problem finding a date. Apparently, according to their chatter, she had been single for a very long time. He had noticed her immediately when he came down the jetway. She was perfect at her job. She made everyone feel welcome as they boarded the plane.

It was her smile that caught him off guard. He had a hard time figuring out how to deal with her cheerful demeanor when he first boarded the airplane. Thinking back, he wished he had been a bit nicer.

He had finally dozed off the last third of the flight but was now paying for the lack of sleep. That's when he decided to make his way to the galley for an early morning coffee, even before they had a chance to offer it to him. He wasn't expecting to see a fresh-faced Emy, leaning so casually against the doorframe, looking incredible.

Emy couldn't have been more than five-five. She had rich, chestnut-brown hair that was swept up in a traditional bun, but it framed her face beautifully. When the light hit her hair just right, it revealed hints of subtle highlights that added depth and dimension.

In that moment, he couldn't tell if her eyes were a shade of green or hazel. Either way, they had flecks of green and brown that seemed to change with the lighting. They held an engaging warmth that he could tell would draw people in.

Her complexion was flawless. Her lips were full and had a soft, inviting quality. When she smiled, it illuminated her entire face. He wasn't sure, but he thought a dimple played on one side of her cheek.

Her perfectly arched eyebrows accentuated her eyes, making them easy to read. Jackson enjoyed this brief moment in which Emy was looking at him. Even though he knew he had stared at her for far too long, he noticed the splatter of freckles across her nose gave her face a youthful look.

As she stood there in her perfectly tailored uniform that accentuated her figure, he wondered if she was aware she was staring back at him.

How long would it have taken her to realize this if it wasn't for her colleague? Something about this made him crack a smile. What he wasn't expecting was the heat he felt when she handed him the coffee he had asked for. And the heat wasn't coming from the coffee. It was only a moment, but a moment that had him scratching his head with a *"What the hell was that?"* feeling.

∞

JACKSON WAS THE YOUNGEST OF FIVE. He had four sisters, so he knew how to treat women and knew eavesdropping was wrong. But from the moment he walked down the jetway, he was curious about the flight attendant who greeted him at the door.

Any other time, he might have made small talk. But tonight, he was irritated. He had been looking forward to spending Christmas Day as the cool uncle to his many nieces and nephews. But apparently, the Paris gallery needed him, and he was the only one "without a significant other." So he had been booked on the first flight out to meet with them the day after Christmas.

Jackson was fully aware of the way his father had said, "No significant commitments keeping you here." Jackson was also aware he was alone, hence the reason he looked forward to being the center of attention with the little crew that didn't look at him with pity but thought he lived a life of leisure and adventure.

He looked forward to pretending they were right. It bothered him to cut the time short, to head home and pack for who knows how long. But that's where he was. In a few minutes, he would land in Paris on Christmas Day. Stores and most restaurants would be closed, and he would once again realize how alone he really was.

5

Emy

"WOULD YOU LIKE BREAKFAST THIS MORNING, MR. RILEY?" Emy was burning up. She could feel the heat radiating off her face.

She wondered if Mr. Riley realized she was standing at his side, holding a placemat over her arm. He hadn't had much to eat during the dinner service, so she assumed he would want some breakfast before they landed in Paris.

"Yes, please." Mr. Riley looked across the aisle at the other flight attendant.

Emy could tell he was wondering why they had changed sides. She looked over in Allen's direction and was certain Mr. Riley caught Allen smirking in their direction. She was at a loss for words. Thankfully, she had done this part of the job for so long, she didn't miss a beat and kept the conversation going.

"We have a lovely French toast and fruit parfait. Can I get you anything other than coffee?" Emy asked.

Jackson seemed as though he could barely answer. "No, thank you. Coffee's great."

As Emy rounded the corner back into the galley, she blurted out, "Allen, I'm going to kill you. This is the most awkward meal service I have ever been part of. And trust me, I've had bad ones before."

"You got this, go get 'em." Allen and Jeff both chuckled as she blew her stray hairs out of her face. "You're doing great. Any minute now he'll open up to you. I can see it." Allen shot her a quick smile before he returned to his side of the cabin.

"Who said I wanted him to open up to me?" Emy gave Allen the once over as she got her tray set up to deliver the meal. She stared at Jeff.

"Don't look at me; I had nothing to do with this one." He had handed off the last meal to Emy and was now starting the cleanup process. He grabbed his coffee and leaned back on the counter as she went back out to the lion's den. He couldn't help but laugh.

Emy didn't get much more out of Mr. Riley. There was an undeniable energy between them. She rarely felt like this, and whatever it was, she didn't like it. She barely managed to pick up his breakfast dishes and make it back to the galley in one piece.

She was relieved the meal service was over. Jeff and Allen got the cabin cleaned up while Emy walked through the other cabins to see if they needed help.

Emy tried to get Chloe's attention, but she was busy getting the economy cabin buttoned up. Emy would have to tell her what happened once they were on the ground.

6

Jackson

TRYING TO CONVINCE HIMSELF THIS WOULD JUST BE A QUICK TRIP IN AND OUT OF PARIS, JACKSON RUBBED HIS EYES. He heard a flight attendant making a standard announcement about landing soon. But he was too groggy to listen.

He looked across the aisle to his fellow passengers in the first row. They had obviously slept much more than he had, and were collecting their belongings.

He ran his hands through his hair, noting that he might need a trim once he got back home, he was distracted by catching a glance of Emy behind the galley curtain.

Just as he started wondering about her, he heard the other female flight attendant checking on a passenger behind him. He turned over his shoulder and was surprised to catch her looking directly down at him.

She finished checking on 2A and scooted up beside him. "Mr. Riley, did you have a good flight?"

She seemed like she was trying hard to keep a professional demeanor. But for some reason, she couldn't keep a straight face. He noticed a subtle smirk on her face like she was up to something more than just confirming his experience.

"I did, thank you." She was still standing beside him. Apparently, she wasn't going away.

She nervously glanced sideways toward the first class galley. She seemed as if she had something else to say. Trying to act as normal as she possibly could, she pivoted in front of him, turning her back to the galley and blocking any potential view he could get of Emy.

"Great, that's good to hear. You know our New York-based crew would love your feedback. There's a comment card in the back of our inflight magazine. I'm happy to give you the names of those who assisted you on your flight today. In fact, I've written it down for your convenience."

She handed him a cocktail napkin with the Infinite Airlines logo embossed on it. In black pen, the name *Emerson Nichols* and a New York phone number was written on it.

Just as the flight attendant straightened up and stepped back, he saw Emy pull back the galley curtain to secure it for landing. She seemed surprised to see her colleague standing there.

Jackson was confused and speechless. But he knew one thing for certain. He now had what appeared to be Emerson's phone number. This routine trip had just gotten interesting.

7

Emy

"YOU... DID... WHAT?"

Emy was at a full standstill in the middle of the Charles de Gaulle terminal when Chloe casually told her she had given Emy's personal number out to a random stranger on the flight.

"No. No, you did not. Oh my gawd, Chloe. What were you thinking?"

Emy didn't know if she was more shocked, embarrassed, or just pissed that Chloe would do such a thing. In all her years of flying, Emy had never once given out her number to a passenger. She had received plenty of numbers from passengers over the years but kept it a one-way street.

It was that one time she gave in and called back a passenger she had met that determined the fate for every passenger after that. Emy realized that when a date with a passenger didn't go well, and they were frequent fliers, things could get awkward. Especially on long flights. It wasn't something she ever planned to do again. She was now chasing after Chloe who kept walking ahead, leaving her standing in the terminal. Chloe wasn't listening to a word Emy was saying.

As she caught up with Chloe, Emy confessed, "I would never do that. You know that."

Emy was still in disbelief that her friend did such a thing. Really, what was she thinking? *Does everyone think I'm so desperate they'd start giving out my phone number like it was Halloween candy?*

Chloe tried not to laugh. "Oh, sweetie, sometimes you just need to throw caution to the wind. I know you'd never do such a thing. So I did it for you. Think of it as living a little outside of your comfortable, cozy box."

Chloe walked with her head held high with long strides, pulling her rolling suitcase behind her like she ruled the world. That was what Emy loved most about Chloe. She was a force. But Chloe was also one to go rogue. Just as she had done on the plane.

"I'm with Chloe," Jeff said. "Live a little. What's the worst that can happen? He calls, you can either answer it, or don't answer, send it to voicemail? Having your number is no big deal. What you do if he calls . . . *that's* a big deal."

"Well, for starters, what if he's a serial killer? Did either of you think of that?"

Emy's anger was slowly dying down, and now fear was settling in. She didn't really think he was a serial killer. There was absolutely no way Jackson Riley would call her. It was Christmas Day in Paris. He obviously had plans, and she was the last person he would be thinking about. She needed to put this out of her mind and think about something else.

But what if he does call? Or worse, what if he doesn't? Now Emy was overthinking her life all over again. Just when she thought she couldn't question anything else, Chloe had added one more thing to her list of questionable choices. How would she let this go?

Emy thought about Christmas as the flight crew made their way through the terminal and out the door to their waiting hotel shuttle. They were in Paris. Half the crew had local friends or family, and would be spending time with them. The van was full of chatter and shared excitement for the day ahead.

As happy as she was in that moment, she also knew this would be her last holiday with Chloe. Next Christmas, Chloe and Patrick would be celebrating together as newlyweds. But for this trip, the girls had a list of things they wanted to do. Top of the list was the Eiffel Tower and the best coffee in the world at Café de la Tartine.

Staying in the heart of Paris at the Hôtel du Louvre was a pleasant surprise. It was a longer layover than usual, so the upgraded hotel was appreciated. The Hôtel du Louvre was one of the first luxury hotels in Paris. It was steps away from the Louvre Museum and Rue St Honoré, one of the best shopping streets in Paris. The famous Jardin des Tuileries was right out-side the door. And if she was lucky, she'd also be able to see the Eiffel Tower from her hotel room window.

Emy looked most forward to a stroll through the pictur-esque Jardin des Tuileries. This time of year, the beautiful gardens would become a busy Christmas fair, turning the gardens into a bustling winter attraction.

Like most of Paris, the famous holiday markets would be closed on Christmas Day, but she couldn't wait to walk through the gardens on her way to the Eiffel Tower. They knew the most popular tourist attraction in Paris would be open, and making their way there would be an adventure. If she couldn't be home, there really was no better place to spend Christmas.

∞

CHECK-IN FOR AN ENTIRE FLIGHT CREW WAS NEVER A QUICK PROCESS. Especially so early in the morning when most rooms weren't available yet. Since Emy and Chloe wanted to be close to each other, they'd be last on the crew list to get their rooms.

Once they were checked in, they made plans to meet in the lobby in an hour. They learned over the years that long naps were never a good idea after checking in, so they wanted to get to their rooms as quickly as possible. Grabbing their bags, they located the elevator and headed in that direction.

"Chloe?" Emy suddenly grabbed Chloe's arm and pulled her back behind a pillar. "Chloe, did you see who just got into the elevator?"

Emy was pulling Chloe further back to ensure no one could see them. The lobby was small. There was no way she could be mistaken.

"No, I didn't. And I won't be able to see anyone else the way you're yanking me."

Chloe started to laugh as she pulled away from Emy to straighten herself back up. She tried to get a look in the direction Emy was talking about. Not seeing anyone else in the cozy lobby, she stepped out and pulled Emy with her.

"There's no one else here, Emy."

"It was Jackson. Mr. Riley. 1A. I'm sure of it." Emy was now using her aggravated, hushed voice. There was no way she could forget his face.

"Emy. You need a nap. We've been standing in this lobby for over thirty minutes waiting for our rooms. We would have seen him if it were him. Maybe it was just someone that looked like him."

Chloe pushed the elevator button. They would just need a quick power nap, time to freshen up, and a bottle of water before heading back downstairs. They didn't have much time and wanted to make the most of the day.

Just when she had gotten him out of her mind, he was right back in it. *Not only is he back, but he's staying at the same hotel! There's no mistaking him. Or is this just wishful thinking?*

8
Jackson

JACKSON HAD WALKED THROUGH CUSTOMS AND WAS LOOKING FOR HIS DRIVER. He knew there was a forty-minute drive into the city ahead of him, and he wanted to get to the hotel so he could shower and rest before reality set in. People would die to be in Paris over the holidays, but this was not where he wanted to be. With no return date scheduled, he was beyond grumpy.

So far, the highlight of the trip was his brief interaction with the cute flight attendant. Reaching into his pocket, he thumbed the cocktail napkin her friend had given him with a name and phone number. *Do I dare use it? Is that crazy?*

He wondered how long she'd be on her layover. If he was going to use it, he had better not think about it too much longer and make the call.

As the car came to a stop, Jackson looked out the window to see the Hôtel du Louvre. Thankfully, he had been booked at a favorite hotel close to the Seine River and the gallery where he'd be spending most of his time.

Once he showered, he would make his way out to the streets of Paris, hoping the Café de la Tartine around the corner would be open on Christmas Day. At least he was in a city he was familiar with and knew his way around. Things could definitely be worse.

As Jackson stepped out of the car, the driver went to the back and pulled Jackson's suitcase out and set it on the curb.

"You are all checked in, sir. Here's your room key. You'll just need to stop by the desk later today to show them your passport."

"Thank you. Merry Christmas!"

Jackson tipped his driver before heading inside. It was nice to be able to bypass the front desk and head straight to his room.

9

Emy

AS PLANNED, EMY WAS DOWNSTAIRS IN THE LOBBY WAITING FOR CHLOE. She knew Chloe was making a few phone calls, so she had a few minutes alone to take in the breathtaking hotel. There was a tiny tree set up in the corner and a cute seating area for two in the front window. Another tree stood tall in the center of the small lobby. But for some reason, it wasn't intrusive.

Emy walked around the tree, looking at its ornaments. Each ornament was filled with a charming winter Parisian scene. Delicate artificial snowflakes rested gently at the bottom of each globe, creating the illusion of freshly fallen snow. She tried to appreciate each one, but she also couldn't let rest that she was certain she had seen Jackson stepping into the elevator earlier.

Looking nothing short of Paris chic, Chloe bounced out of the elevator, heading Emy's way. Her blonde hair contrasted with the red beret she had resting on her perfect loose curls that framed her face.

"Ready to go?" Chloe was putting on a fresh coat of lip gloss as they walked toward the door.

The girls stepped out of their hotel into the cold Paris morning. They were greeted by a scene that seemed straight out of a romantic movie. Since most of Paris had celebrated Christmas with family the evening before, the streets were alive and welcoming as people headed toward their next gathering with friends. Emy loved their tradition of spending Christmas Eve with family, then Christmas Day with friends.

"Oh comme j'aime Paris," Emy exclaimed.

She really did love Paris. The air was crisp and biting, with a hint of frost. It was almost like the city was daring it to snow. Arm in arm, they stepped out onto the curb, heading toward their favorite café. Fingers crossed that it would be open.

Emy cinched her coat tighter and felt the warmth of the scarf against her neck. Her breath formed delicate clouds in the chilly air. As the two walked side by side down the cobbled streets, their heeled boots echoed softly against the pavement. They linked arms, not only for support and warmth but also as two sisters giggling down the street. She no longer felt alone, but alive.

As the two walked down the street, everyone was out, enjoying the beautiful Paris morning. Luckily, the café was open, and several others were already inside, enjoying it as well. Several empty outdoor tables invited customers to sit, but Emy and Chloe wanted to sit inside, out of the cold.

Emy pulled the door open and started to step inside. But immediately stopped short. Chloe smacked right into her back, pushing both girls inside the door.

"Oh, mon, what are you doing?" Chloe was still trying to regain her composure when she looked around Emy.

Before Chloe could speak, Emy had them turned around and headed out the door.

"Oh no you don't!" Chloe grabbed her by the arm, forcing her back inside again. "Go! Move it. Don't make this any weirder than you already have."

Chloe instantly saw what, or actually who, had made Emy turn around in the other direction.

Sitting at a table inside the café was none other than Jackson Riley. She *had* seen him in the hotel, and now he was sitting in her favorite café. Jackson was probably trying not to laugh at the scene they were causing.

Chloe leaned into her ear and whispered, "Emy, we have two choices here. We can leave and look like fools. Or we can walk over and say hello."

Chloe was already pulling Emy over in his direction. She wasn't giving her any time to think about her options.

"Well, hello, Mr. 1A, we meet again!" Chloe deposited Emy in the chair directly across from Jackson, then grabbed her own seat next to them.

Emy's eyes were the size of saucers.

"What are the odds we would see you again so soon? Emy, aren't we surprised to see Mr. 1A again so soon?"

Realizing Chloe was not going to let up, she made herself as comfortable as she could be given the current situation. Emy took off her gloves and unwrapped her scarf from her neck. She could only imagine how this would go.

"Hello," Emy greeted, timidly.

Chloe always got them into trouble. Emy was normally the one who got them *out* of trouble. But for the first time, she was at a loss.

"Ladies, nice to see you. And it's Jackson. My name is Jackson. I think that's probably better than any name you've come up with for me so far." He sat back and took a sip of his espresso.

"Care to join me?" he asked casually, as if they hadn't already invaded his space.

Before any of them could say anything, Chloe excused herself to order their drinks. Emy and Chloe had been roommates and travel partners for so long, there was no need to ask what Emy wanted. In Paris, there were few options anyway. At Café de la Tartine, it would be nothing less than a cappuccino for each of them.

Jackson sat across from Emy, not saying a word. But she was sure he was laughing with his eyes.

"Did I see you get into the elevator at the hotel this morning?" she asked.

"Well, that depends. In what hotel would I have been taking this elevator?" he tried to clarify. "I mean, there are hundreds of hotels in Paris."

He was gazing intently into her eyes.

"It would be careless of me to tell you where your flight crew was staying."

She looked around for Chloe. Why was that girl taking so long? She really needed something to do with her hands. As she sat with this gorgeous man, her stomach turned into knots.

Emy couldn't remember the last time she felt this way. She tried her best to seem casual. For some reason, Jackson's sudden appearance had her falling apart on the inside. She was hoping he couldn't tell just by looking at her.

"Here you go, Emy." Chloe set down the beautiful cappuccino on top of a small, delicately patterned saucer.

The cappuccino was more of a work of art than a plain cup of coffee. The froth had a subtle floral design that added to its charm. Just as she picked up the small cup to put it to her lips, she realized Chloe didn't have any coffee of her own.

"Hey, you know what? It's now Christmas back home. I'm going to give Patrick a call. You two enjoy yourselves, and Emy, can we meet back at the hotel in an hour or so?"

Before Emy knew what was happening, Chloe was out the door, leaving her at the cozy table for two with Jackson Riley. Looking over her shoulder, Chloe blew a kiss in their direction.

Emy was seething.

10

Jackson

JACKSON LOOKED ACROSS THE TABLE, TRYING TO FIGURE OUT
IF EMY WAS GOING TO STAY OR GO. Right now, she looked as
though she couldn't leave fast enough. Really hoping she'd stay,
he did his best to make things less awkward for her.

"You know, it's funny how Christmas in Paris can be both
magical and lonely at the same time. I don't think we've officially met yet. I'm Jackson Riley." Setting down his espresso, he
reached across the table, offering his hand.

"Emerson Nichols. And we just got bamboozled by my
former roommate and best friend, Chloe."

Jackson noted her smile, and realized she was still holding his hand.

"It's very nice to meet you, Jackson Riley. Officially, that is."

He wasn't going to be the first to let her hand go. He realized she wasn't going to let go either. Her touch was warm and reassuring. In that moment, they both realized that this newfound connection with a stranger in a Paris café might be far more meaningful than either of them could have imagined. It was as if their hands bridged the gap between their solitude, filling the space with a sense of comfort and understanding that words alone could not describe.

"So, Emerson Nichols, does your friend normally pawn you off with strangers on Christmas Day?" This time, there was humor in his voice.

Emy gently pulled her hand back into her lap. Sensing she had been a little tense up to this point, he was glad to see her finally starting to relax.

"Former friend. And no, this is a first for both of us." she snickered as she put her coffee to her lips.

Jackson couldn't take his eyes off her. She had a glow that lit up the room, and he was in awe of her presence. Despite her apparent nervousness, she still carried herself with grace and ease.

He hadn't felt any Christmas spirit until he saw Emy. Of course, he had seen her try to escape when she noticed him sitting there. But it was more than their awkward entry that turned every head in the café their way. Both girls knew how to demand the attention of everyone in the room.

"I don't know." He paused, looking directly into Emy's eyes. "If it wasn't for her, you wouldn't be sitting here with me right now."

She laughed out loud. He was right. Had she been alone, there was no way she would joined him in the café, even if she had wanted to. Jackson was quite pleased, sitting here with her.

Emy confessed, "You're right. I probably wouldn't be."

He watched her closely as she finished the last sips of her cappuccino.

Setting down her cup, "So, Jackson Riley. What brings you to Paris on Christmas morning?"

She picked up her spoon to try to get the last little bit of foam from her now empty cappuccino cup.

"Work. I have a meeting tomorrow with the Musée d'art Moderne. We have a small family gallery back home, and we're acquiring several pieces for an upcoming show. Someone needed to be here for the transfer tomorrow."

Jackson looked around the café. He noticed several other patrons sitting alone and wondered how they ended up here on Christmas Day.

"It was supposed to be one of my sisters. But the date was moved up unexpectedly. Since I don't have any commitments per se, here I am."

11

Emy

IN THE SHORT TIME SHE HAD BEEN SITTING WITH JACKSON, EMY COULD TELL HE WAS SAD TO BE FAR AWAY FROM HIS FAMILY. She was used to holidays alone. Ever since she was little, holidays were just another day around her house.

Her mother was a flight attendant, and her father was a pilot. It was a total cliché and another reason why she would never again cross the line with passengers or flight crew. Emy loved her parents deeply and had an amazing childhood. But she wanted something more for her life. They had always been on the go. She was sure that's where she got the unsettled feeling she was experiencing now.

While the constant travel and unconventional schedules defined her family's lifestyle, Emy fondly recalled the exciting tales her parents brought home from their journeys, transforming her home into a treasure trove of global experiences. Her upbringing instilled in her a love for diversity and a curiosity about the world beyond her immediate surroundings. It inspired her to follow in her mother's footsteps.

Yet alongside the thrill of exploration, she acknowledged the challenges of holidays spent without traditional family gatherings. A bittersweet reminder of the sacrifices woven into the fabric of her parents' professions.

"That must be tough, being away. Not that I'd know. I've never been home for Christmas or most holidays, come to think about it." Emy paused, tapping her spoon on the side of her empty cup, then setting it down on the saucer. "Both my parents worked for Infinite Airlines. We traveled a lot, but it was just the three of us."

The more she spoke, this started to sound depressing to her. She needed to change the subject. Not wanting to discuss more travel life, Emy asked, "Do you have plans for the rest of the day? I need to head back to the hotel to grab Chloe, but I'd love for you to walk back with me."

Emy was already standing, putting on her coat.

Jackson stood as well. Even with her boots, he was still almost a full head taller than she was. His hair was tamer than it had been at the end of the flight but still looked intentionally messy. He was exceptionally fit, and she could see his toned arms through his fitted sweater.

Thinking about him this way, as he stood right in front of her made her blush. Catching herself, she shook her head to refocus.

"Shall we go?" Emy asked as she headed toward the door. Before exiting the café, she typed out a quick text to Chloe…

> **EMY** So going to kill you. Later. But for now coming back to hotel. Meet me in the lobby so we can head out.

Although Emy had traveled the world alone for years, she had never met up with someone she didn't know. For some reason, she felt comfortable with Jackson.

As they stepped outside the café, the two were hit with a cold breeze that had picked up. She wrapped her scarf around her neck and tucked it into her coat. She noticed Jackson had tucked his hands in his pocket but otherwise seemed unfazed by the cold temperatures.

For the first few steps, they walked in silence. *Is this crazy? Is he just as apprehensive about this as I am? Who does this?* Before she had time for another thought, Emy was surprised when she felt his hand slip into hers.

"How are you so sure we're at the same hotel?" he smiled.

Emy realized she had never confirmed that he was at the Hôtel du Louvre. But there was no way she was mistaken. Especially after ending up at the same café, just blocks away.

Looking straight ahead, Jackson flirtatiously admitted, "I'm cold, and I forgot my gloves. Your hand will have to do." A confident smirk appeared on his face for the first time.

They chuckled and kept walking. Emy held his hand tightly—something that surprised even her.

"As long as that's all it is!"

She couldn't remember the last time someone had held her hand like this. It was casual, but it generated a lot of heat between them. She couldn't be the only one feeling this.

"And I rarely forget a face. I knew I saw you in our lobby."

She didn't tell him how she and Chloe had hidden out of sight, not wanting to be seen as he stepped into the elevator.

The hotel was just minutes away, so the walk was short. Too short even. There was something about him that made her want to know more.

As they rounded the corner, they had suddenly arrived at the hotel. Walking up the front steps to the hotel, Emy let go of his hand. The last thing she needed was Chloe or any other crew member seeing her holding hands with Mr. 1A.

As they entered the lobby, Emy looked around for Chloe. She was nowhere in sight. She pulled out her phone and sent her another quick text.

EMY I'm waiting!

The hotel lobby was quiet. However, the cozy ambiance, Parisian flare, soft lighting, and the enormous Christmas tree all made it exceptionally warm and inviting. As she turned around and looked for her friend, Emy whispered, "I wonder where she is. She's never on time. I messaged her fifteen minutes ago."

Jackson nodded, and with a grin on his face, he offered, "Maybe she's stuck in the elevator. Or still on the phone."

Emy wasn't sure why Jackson thought this was funny. It was as though he knew something she didn't.

He continued waiting with Emy. Standing in the lobby, unsure what to do, she felt her phone buzz.

> **CHLOE** Not feeling great, go ahead without me. I'm sure I'll be fine for dinner!

Emy shoved her phone into her handbag. *Not feeling good? Yah. Right!*

She had known Chloe for years, and this was exactly something Chloe would do. Chloe was notorious for getting them into sticky situations. Emy was always the one who had to get them out. Chloe really needed to stop this.

But am I really mad about it?

∞

"EVERYTHING OKAY?" Jackson studied her intensely.

How quickly plans have changed. With the turn of events, Emy realized she had a choice to make. She could spend the day by herself, or invite Jackson to come along with her. She would never waste away a day in Paris. Plus, she had reservations that she was looking forward to.

"Well. How would you like to take Chloe's place today? Apparently, she's feeling under the weather. That's assuming you don't already have plans and want to hang out with a complete stranger."

Emy felt the rush of heat go straight to her cheeks. She had never been so forward. She had a full day planned, and was excited about the prospect of spending more time with him. The short amount of time at the café had left her wanting more.

She tried to read Jackson's thoughts. Judging by what little she knew of him, she guessed that everything he did was probably planned out and calculated.

"Well, technically we're not complete strangers. We've officially known each other for about an hour now." She tried to ditch the sarcasm attached to her invitation.

He cracked a smile. "Sure, I'd love to be Chloe for the day. It just so happens, I'm free until tomorrow morning. My only plans were to check in with my family at some point today."

"What are we doing first?" he asked as they walked toward the door.

Emy gleefully took Jackson's hand as though they'd known each other forever. They went outside as the mid-morning sun cast a warm, golden hue over the walkway leading to the Tuileries. She wanted to walk through the gardens on their way to the Eiffel Tower.

They strolled hand in hand through the gardens, just like other couples around them. The gardens were donned with decorations left over from the Christmas market. Small booths that had been full of crafts and local treats just the day before were still standing, but abandoned for Christmas Day. Now, in the quiet aftermath of the market, the reindeer sets created a nostalgic glow, a reminder of festive cheer and the warmth of holiday gatherings. They stood poised and ready, their lights still twinkling softly against the winter morning. Although the market was closed, the gardens were still full of people walking all around.

"Thank you for coming out with me. Although I'm sure you figured out that Chloe is not really sick. This is just her way of trying to set us up."

Emy thought it was best to get the truth out there and out of the way. She really wasn't upset with Chloe. After all, she was spending the day with this gorgeous man she'd just met. Jackson had been nothing less than polite and well-mannered. At no time had Emy felt uneasy with him.

"Feel free to make something up any time, take a fake call, whatever you have to do to get out of this date." As they walked, he had yet to release her hand.

"So, it's a date, huh?" Jackson gave her a concerned look before giving her a gentle tug toward him. Emy blushed.

"You know what I mean." She bit her lip. She liked the idea of this being a date. "But if we are going to be calling this a date, I hope you're ready to be wowed. I had an amazing time planned with Chloe today!"

She was surprised Chloe would toss the day away so Emy could galivant around Paris with Jackson. She had really wanted to spend the day with her friend, but it was everyone's mission to set her up with any guy who showed interest in her.

As they continued through the gardens, hand in hand, puffs of their breath hung in the frosty air as they strolled along the tree-lined pathways. The crunch of footsteps on the pebbled path beneath their feet provided a soothing rhythm. A light dusting of snow adorned the sculpted hedges and statues, adding an extra layer of charm to the urban landscape surrounding them.

Emy's cheeks flushed with a rosy glow from the freezing temperature. The color of her cheeks matched her scarf. Her gloved hand was still in Jackson's.

She smiled up at him, surprised by how happy she was. Jackson was very handsome; she couldn't help but steal glances at him as they made small talk along the way. Once she got past Chloe's deception, she felt a deep sense of contentment. It was lovely to be out and about in Paris on Christmas Day.

"Tell me, Jackson Riley, where do you live?" She already knew he was single and lived somewhere in Manhattan. "Wait, don't tell me, let me guess. You seem like a Tribeca kinda guy."

Emy giggled like she knew him better than he had thought but was trying not to insult him in the process.

"What makes you so sure about that?" He had been smiling since they left the hotel.

"Your effortless Jake Gyllenhaal look." Emy answered. "In fact, I bet you hang out with him. I can see you strolling down Chambers Street with your fancy coffee, talking about the previous night's Knicks game."

She was still revelling in her description when Jackson stopped abruptly, pulling her back into him.

He looked right into Emy's eyes. "You think you're funny, don't you?" There was a long, lingering pause. He stared down at her for what seemed like an eternity. Clearing his throat, he pulled her back to the side and started walking again.

"For the record, I don't live in Tribeca. I live in the West Village." Without missing a beat, he quipped, "I have coffee with Bradley Cooper, not Jake Gyllenhaal."

They both laugh. However, Emy wasn't so sure if he was serious or not. Jackson was obviously from money. She, on the other hand, had inherited her West Village apartment from her parents. It was really on loan as they traveled the world. She had hoped that one day they would finally decide to give it to her so she could feel like she really belonged. It was the apartment she grew up in, and the worry of her parents selling it was always in the back of her mind. It was small, but it worked for her.

"Tell me, where do flight attendants live?" Jackson looked at her curiously.

"All flight attendants? Or just me?" Emy was flirting, and she knew it. "It looks like we might be neighbors?" Somehow, saying that out loud was both scary and exciting. All logic was wholly lost on her. She was telling a stranger where she lived and holding his hand.

She felt relaxed as they walked through the gardens, passing the Bassin Octogonal fountain. It wasn't just that Jackson was easy on the eyes; he had a warmth about him. Emy never would have guessed that by their first meeting. But walking with him now, she could tell he was the type of guy everyone wanted to be around.

"Not surprised." Jackson tightened his grip and moved a little closer to her. "That fits you. How long have you lived there?"

"Well, to be fair, my whole life. It's my parent's apartment that they've abandoned for a life of leisure. They both retired from Infinite and have been on the go ever since. Chloe and I have been living there now for years. Until recently, that is."

Emy suddenly remembered why it was so important for her to spend the day with Chloe. Although she quickly reminded herself how happy she was for Chloe, she was still sad that her friend was moving on. She knew they wouldn't be roommates forever, but she was going to miss her terribly. Chloe had stayed with her boyfriend, Patrick, more and more the last few months. When they got engaged, she officially moved in with him.

As the two made their way down the garden path, they talked almost as though they were long lost friends. Being with

Jackson was nice. Holding his hand was comfortable, something she didn't realize she had been missing.

"Funny that we've never run into each other in the Village. I would have remembered you for sure."

Emy looked straight ahead. Every time she looked his way, she felt a flutter in her stomach. Something she hadn't felt in a very long time.

In fact, the last time she held someone's hand had to be well over two years ago. She was not one to maintain relationships. She was gone a lot, and she had never met anyone that would make her want to stay home long enough to see if it would work out. She loved her life, but as her friends started to settle down, she felt like she was missing out on something more.

"Really? What makes me so memorable?" Jackson seemed genuinely curious to hear what she thought of him.

Emy paused for a second. She envisioned him walking down the streets of the West Village. He had an unforgettable face.

"You're tall with messy hair. I'd see that hair coming a mile away." She laughed, then got quiet.

Thinking about her life, Emy felt restless, which rarely happened. She wasn't sure if it was the holiday season or all the changes around her. Perhaps she had seen Jackson in the Village at some point but just missed noting him in the bustle of life.

"Yes, definitely your messy hair for sure. Very memorable."

Emy was more playful today than she had been in a while. Apparently, Jackson was bringing out joy that she worried wasn't surfacing much anymore.

12

Jackson

"YOU STILL HAVEN'T TOLD ME WHAT OUR PLANS ARE FOR THE DAY." Jackson smirked at Emy.

He felt completely at ease with her. She was fun, had a great smile, and something about her made him feel good. He had no intentions of leaving the hotel today, but here he was, spending the day with this incredible woman.

He felt more relaxed and confident. Nothing like he had been the day before. If someone told him then that he'd be spending the day with this amazing woman, he never would have believed it. He had been stressed out about coming to Paris alone over Christmas. Leaving his family behind didn't help. But hopefully spending the day together would make being away from them a little easier.

"Well, my friend, I hope you're ready for the ultimate Paris tourist experience."

"As I was planning this trip, I knew most everything would be closed on Christmas Day. So I had carefully plotted out a fun day of activities and places that I knew would be open. Get ready, our first stop is coming up. I hope you're excited about being a tourist with me today."

Emy stopped in her tracks. Just ahead of them was the glorious Eiffel Tower.

"I hope you're not afraid of heights Mr. Riley. We're not just visiting one of the most famous landmarks in Paris. I have a surprise for you once we get up there."

Jackson clapped his hands together. "Fantastic, a Paris classic. I love it."

He wasn't used to having too many days off. And when he did have free time, playing tourist was not at the top of his list.

"I hope you still feel that way by the end of the day." She was eager to see his reaction. "When was the last time you went up the Tower?"

He paused for a second, then looked over at Emy. "You know, I've never been up there before. I've walked by, I don't know, a hundred times, but I've never actually taken time to go up."

He kept looking up at the Tower.

"I'm embarrassed. I've been to Paris countless times over the last ten years. How can I have passed the Eiffel Tower and never taken the time to explore it? Maybe it's because I'm usually alone. If I had someone to explore it with, maybe I would have been to the top by now."

Emy seemed surprised. "What? You can't be serious. Not even at night?"

The Eiffel Tower was home to one of the best open-air ice skating rinks in the world. It was small and exclusive to those with tickets to the Tower and had one of the best views of the city. Emy was excited to experience this with him. She started walking faster, pulling Jackson with her.

Jackson let Emy pull him along, leading the way. The lines were long, but she had already purchased tickets well in advance. He knew she wanted to experience this with her friend, so he was determined to make this memorable for both of them. And it was true, he had been by the Tower countless times but had never actually stepped foot inside the Tower itself. He had never even been this close.

As she led them forward, he noted she had been here often. A tourist, she was not.

"Stay here, I'll be back in a minute."

Emy left Jackson standing in the center of the Tower base while she checked them in. He gazed upward; his neck craned to take in the sheer height of the structure. The intricate lattice of ironwork created a captivating display of lights and shadows, especially when the sun hit it at different angles. The Tower stood tall against the sky, with its elegant curves and geometric patterns. The enormity of the structure left him in awe.

Jackson felt Emy return before he even heard her. "You're right. I can't believe I haven't done this before."

He turned and looked for her hand. He had missed holding her hand while she had been gone. It wasn't just the cold; he wanted to be close to her. As he took Emy's hand again, she didn't even flinch.

With a wide grin, she looked at Jackson. For the first time all day, he seemed a little unsure. Little did he know, she was going to be relying on him a lot in the coming minutes. Maybe he should be more concerned.

"You, Jackson Riley, are in for it."

Emy led him to the elevator. Soon, they were on their way up the Tower. Jackson was a little surprised when they stopped at the first level. The doors opened and several others piled out, disappearing in different directions. He followed her as she looked around the open-air level and headed in the direction of a counter on the far left. A temporary sign overhead at the counter read, *Skate Box.*

Jackson let out a nervous laugh as he looked around the first floor of the Tower. How he missed it when he exited the elevator, he didn't know. Just to the right, there was a sparkling ice skating rink. Now the skate rental sign made sense. He hadn't been this excited since he was a little kid. He was going skating with Emy 200 feet above the ground, and he couldn't have planned anything better than this for Christmas Day.

"Wow, the view is amazing. Best view in the city."

Emy moved quickly and efficiently so he didn't have time to object. She had barely taken a breath. "I have wanted to do this for so long. I bought tickets in case Chloe made the trip with me."

She asked the man at the counter for shoes in a size thirty-seven. "What's your size, Jackson?"

Jackson had looked back at Emy. He told her his shoe size and took them from the man at the counter. The two of them found a spot on a secure bench, sat down, and started to lace up. They were really doing this.

"Am I safe to assume that, living in New York, you've ice skated before?"

He had wanted to tell her that he'd been skating for years, but seeing how excited she was, thinking that he might struggle a bit, he decided to wait until they were on the ice to show off his skills.

"Yes, I've skated before, but to be honest? I have no idea when the last time was." He knew exactly when it was—every winter in Central Park. Those winters were filled with countless memories of skating with his sisters during the holidays in New York.

"Growing up in New York City, we had plenty of opportunities to go ice skating each winter. My family made the trek to Central Park each Christmas. It was a tradition for as long as I can remember. I'm not sure when we stopped going."

Giving his laces one final pull, he stood up and reached for Emy's hand. "Ready for this?"

13

Emy

NOTHING COULD HAVE PREPARED EMY FOR HER TIME ICE SKATING WITH JACKSON. He was graceful, confident, and great at ice skating. She, on the other hand, was trying hard not to fall.

Apparently, skating wasn't like riding a bike. As she shuffled her way around the rink, she was doing all she could to stay upright. She hadn't been on the ice in years. Walking by Rockefeller Center and looking at the skaters was definitely not the same as being one of the skaters.

Jackson let go of Emy's hand and spun around in front of her. The two were face to face as he continued to skate backward. For a moment, she lost her balance and threw out her arms to avoid falling. He moved in closer and took both of her hands.

"Here, let me help you." Jackson looked deep into Emy's eyes, smiling down at her as he guided her around the rink with ease.

"Admit it. You're a professional ice skater, aren't you?" She tightened her grip and began moving at his pace. She was confident he wouldn't let her fall. If she did, she was sure he'd go down with her, just to make her feel better. That's the kind of guy she got the feeling Jackson Riley was.

"Ha, not a professional, no. However, I told you I have four sisters and several nieces and nephews, right? I might not have been completely truthful when I said I didn't know when the last time I had gone skating."

Then Jackson spun her unexpectedly toward the center of the rink.

The two were now in the center of the rink, moving in a tight circle.

"Last winter for sure. And maybe every winter before that."

He now led Emy at a comfortable pace as they made their way around the inner circle of the rink. They skated in silence for a few more minutes before he slowed to a brief stop. He looked over at Emy, who breathed heavily but still managed to stay on her feet. She took a deep breath in and out as she wiped her hair from her face.

"Honestly, every time I put ice skates on, I'm surprised I can still manage my way around the rink. And if I'm being honest? I've never been more grateful. I can't imagine what you'd think of me if I couldn't hold my own right now."

They spent a good chunk of the morning on the rink. Jackson made Emy feel like a better skater than she was. The two skated effortlessly around the rink, enjoying the view and laughing at the possibility that with each curve of the rink, they could fall on the ice.

They slowly came to a stop on the side of the rink. He stood there for several seconds, taking in the surroundings. "Since you paid for skating, the least I can do is cover hot chocolate. How does that sound?"

Before she could respond, Jackson pulled her to the rink exit. "To be honest, I'm not sure how much longer I would have lasted. I wanted to stop before my luck ran out."

Emy was freezing. She was relieved to hear his confession as they exited the rink.

As they walked around families just arriving to take to the ice, Emy and Jackson made their way over to a café beside the rink. As the sun warmed the rest of Paris, the Eiffel Tower grew busier. They were lucky to grab one of the two tables left. Jackson returned to the table after ordering two cups of decadent hot chocolate.

"For you, madame," Jackson said as he set the cup in front of her. Before he sat down, he moved his chair closer to her. For a moment, they sat in silence. She was unsure how long Jackson would sit with her. Maybe this was where the day would end.

"Thank you! Thank you for letting me drag you with me on my Paris adventure today. This is something I've wanted to do for so long. I see the people out here at Christmas and always thought it would be romantic to be here."

Emy raised her cup and took a sip of the warm chocolate. She hadn't realized how cold she was and was grateful to have the drink to warm her up.

As she leaned in closer, a warm, subtle fragrance ignited her senses.

Jackson caught a hint of her movement and turned to meet her gaze. "Are you smelling me?"

Emy practically choked on her chocolate. "I was. And I am not ashamed to admit it either," she said with a nervous laugh. She had no intention of admitting to him that she enjoyed how he smelled, but apparently, she got caught.

Their eyes locked for a moment, and a gentle smile played on Jackson's lips. The air between them was thinning, and Emy felt another soft flutter in her stomach. She inhaled again, savoring the scent that seemed to be uniquely his—a blend of musky cologne and a hint of something sweet. She assumed it was the hot chocolate. Her heart quickened.

Without a word, Jackson reached out, moving the strands of hair hanging down in her face. He tucked the strands behind her ear as if he wanted a better look at her.

The electricity of their touch made Emy shiver. The world seemed to fade away, leaving only the two of them sitting outside the café of the Eiffel Tower.

As he leaned in closer, Emy could feel the warmth of Jackson's breath on her skin. She stopped breathing, as the air was charged with anticipation. As their lips met in a delicate, lingering kiss, they found a shared rhythm and an unspoken need. The warmth of his lips sent heat through her body.

How incredibly easy it was to get lost in a few split seconds. She leaned in and moved closer to make the kiss last even longer. Then she pulled back as the sheer shock of what she was doing hit her like a blast of cold wind.

Jackson didn't move. Instead, he looked deeper into her eyes, and cracked his trademark smile. "I hope this doesn't mean our date is over. I'm looking forward to what's next."

"Oh, this date is far from over." Emy surprised herself at how quickly she responded. She stood up and reached out her hand. "Are you coming?"

She wasn't sure how much of the day she had been smiling. Just a few hours earlier, she was questioning her life decisions. Now, she was spending the day in Paris with Jackson Riley from New York.

She had a feeling Chloe was doing just fine back at the hotel, binge-watching her favorite Netflix show. Emy certainly could not be mad at Chloe right now. They both seemed to be exactly where they were supposed to be.

14

Jackson

"I HAVE TO WARN YOU," EMY SAID, TURNING TO LOOK UP AT HIM. "Today's itinerary is for nomads. Chloe and I are so used to being on the road during the holidays. What may seem normal to us might not be for you in the traditional holday sense."

"Well, so far, nothing about today has been very traditional."

"I've been looking forward to what's next all day. When I'm in Paris, I love strolling down the Champs-Élysées. Are you up for a walk?"

In New York, the subway was his typical way of getting around, but he loved walking the streets of Paris.

"I'm a New Yorker; that question is almost offensive." Jackson walked faster to show her he could easily keep pace with her.

As they slowly walked the path that led them toward the Seine, Emy took a deep breath of the cold, brisk air.

"What would you be doing today if you were home?"

Jackson pulled his jacket closed and tightened his scarf. It was getting colder, even though the sun was shining bright. It was the most captivating Christmas morning Paris could offer. Kids rode new bikes along the river, parents pushed strollers, and others made their way to wherever it was they'd spend the rest of the day. It was magical and made him long for home.

He was usually an extremely private person, but he felt like he could tell her anything.

"Christmas morning is always at my sister, Juliette's house. She has the most kids, so it's easiest for all of us to end up there. But it takes a while for all of us to get there since she's in Brooklyn."

"My parents usually spend the night at Juliette's. Jade and Jordan also have kids, so they get there earlier too. Jessica isn't married and doesn't have kids either. Since we don't have the same amount of responsibilities as our oldest sisters, we entertain the kids. They're great. They're the last humans on earth that think I'm cool. And I'm not sure how much longer that'll last as they get older."

"I'm usually last to arrive. That way, my sisters have time to give me a list of things they've forgotten and need before I arrive. It's efficient. I don't have to go back out to get them, and I get to make a grand entrance. I think there's about twenty of us by now."

Jackson thought about each one of his family members.

"As much as I'm going to miss my family today, my sisters are going to be sorry that I'm not with them. Normally, I run interference. But this year, they're on their own. They have Jessica, but she's a little rough around the edges. Uptight might be the right word."

He started to laugh.

"Yep, I almost feel sorry for Jessica. It's not going to be easy on her. I'm definitely the favorite of the bunch. They need me to keep the kids occupied. I can't wait to hear all about it when I get home."

As they walked, Emy looked up at Jackson as he talked about his family. "I'm sorry you're not with them today. I can tell how much you love your family. I wish I could be part of something like that."

"What about you? If you weren't on a layover, where would you be?" he asked.

"Honestly? I have worked every Christmas since my parents retired. We don't have a big family; it's just me and my parents. I don't think we have ever had what you described, not even close actually. It's always just been the three of us."

"But I don't feel like I've missed out. I guess I just don't know any different, and I accepted my life years ago. Besides, if I work Christmas Day, someone else can stay home for the holiday."

"What about your parents?"

"My parents always invited me to join them wherever they were, but it was usually someplace far away. I love that my parents travelled so much. Now that they're in their late sixties, they're finally settling down. I'm happy for them."

Emy continued explaining to him, "I love the unpredictability and new adventures that come my way. I don't know what it's like to have a big family and the chaos that comes with it. But I've never felt like I was missing out."

"You don't mind being alone?"

"I've never thought about it as being alone. Especially when I'm working. But I guess you're right."

Emy looked around as if she was trying to find something. "And I hadn't really thought too much about it until recently, but my life isn't exactly what most people would consider normal."

She pulled Jackson across the street as they approached the Flame of Liberty. She navigated the streets of Paris like a local. "If I hadn't travelled so much in the last twelve years, I wouldn't know my way around so well."

15

Emy

"Look, one of the best views of the Eiffel Tower, and we get to celebrate friendship with the flame."

Emy pulled off her gloves and pulled her phone out of her pocket. Without hesitating, she clicked a quick selfie of the two of them.

"Sometimes I can't get to the Eiffel Tower, but I at least come here."

She knew her way around Paris just as well as she did her own home streets in the West Village. She also knew exactly where they were going next, and she hoped Jackson loved crepes as much as she did.

Tucked away in the eighth arrondissement, Emy had found one of the best creperies in the city. It was just steps away from the buzzing streets, the trendy museums, and shopping districts. C'est Délicieux Crêperie had the best ham and cheese buckwheat galettes in the city. As she thought about it, her mouth watered.

Emy turned to Jackson, furrowing her brow.

"I'm about to share one of my best kept secrets with you. You have to promise not to tell anyone."

She held up her pinky, demanding a pinky promise before sharing secrets with him. Jackson started to laugh.

"I'm serious. I don't even share this place with crewmembers. I don't want it to become the next TikTok trend. I don't like to wait in lines, so let's keep this place to ourselves, please."

Jackson rocked back on his heels and looked up at the sky before he hooked his pinky with hers. "Okay, I'm trusting you. Let's go."

Then she led the way down a tiny alley off the Rue de la Paix, where C'est Délicieux Crêperie was tucked away. Emy had first learned of the creperie after a late night out, several years ago on a layover with Chloe. They had stumbled upon a creperie stall and devoured what they considered "drunk food" at the time. Years later, she was happy to have found a full sit-down creperie that had spun off from the famous stall.

Shedding their coats, Jackson pulled out a chair for her to sit in. She hadn't felt this at ease in a long time. She didn't want this feeling to end.

Emy ordered a ham and cheese galette and a salted butter caramel crepe for them to share.

"It's Christmas. Shall we have some champagne too?"

"We're in Paris, aren't we?"

She could tell Jackson was going along with it all. This was supposed to be part of her day with Chloe. Emy sensed he didn't want to disappoint her in any way, and the thought made her feel warm all over.

"Champagne is always a good idea, right?" She picked up her glass and held it out to Jackson. "Merry Christmas." She lifted the glass to her lips, but never looked away from Jackson.

Emy had looked forward to this part for the trip the most. No other place in the States could come close to what they experienced. She savored each bite.

The two spent the next hour chatting about Emy's life as the only daughter of nontraditional parents. Emy was an unexpected surprise. When she came along, her parents decided to raise her differently. They were movers. Travelers at heart.

With her father as a pilot and her mother as a flight attendant for Infinite Airlines, Emy had a vast appreciation of her surroundings, no matter where she landed. She took advantage of every travel experience that came her way. Not every travel experience had been perfect, but those rough spots made her the easygoing person she was. She learned early on that sometimes she had to expect the unexpected.

∞

"OKAY, TOTALLY UNDERSTAND WHY WE NEED TO KEEP THAT PLACE A SECRET." Jackson put on his gloves as he walked out onto the cobblestone street. "Delicious. Best creperie hands down. I fully agree… there's nothing comparable in New York."

"I told you," Emy said. "It's a gem for sure. And thank you. You really didn't have to pick up the check."

Emy was walking along the street with Jackson when she linked her arm through his. It wasn't as cold now, so she couldn't pretend it was for any reason other than because she wanted to be close to him. He didn't seem to mind, and moved in closer to her.

"Hey, where'd you get those gloves? I thought you left them back at the hotel?" She was still holding his arm tight but had a smile on her face.

Jackson gazed down at Emy. "I lied. I just wanted to hold your hand." Before she could respond, he changed the subject, "Good views, great crepes. What are we doing next?"

As they walked, she noticed how nicely Jackson was dressed. She was sure he'd enjoy the next part of the plan, based on his expensive loafers and appreciation of art.

Emy looked forward to walking down the Champs-Élysées. Many of the stores and restaurants would be closed, but the street would be lit up with twinkling Christmas lights. It would almost be more enjoyable now, with less of the hustle and bustle of a normal day.

"I'm not sure you'll want to join me. It's a lot of walking"

Looking around, she could see a metro stop just up the street. It would be easy for him to hop on and head back to the hotel from where they were.

Before she had time to suggest the metro ride back to the hotel, Jackson moved in close to Emy, taking her face in his hands, and kissed her. Her eyes, reflecting a mixture of surprise and a hint of excitement, met his gaze. Everything around them blurred.

Their lips met in a soft, tender collision. The kiss was meant to be gentle, but the longer their lips stayed connected, the more excitement she felt for Jackson. He moved his hand into her hair and tilted her head, deepening their kiss.

She felt a brush of warmth that sent a shiver down her spine. In that moment, she realized it was more than just a kiss. She could feel his signal that he wanted to be there with her. He wasn't going anywhere.

Without stepping away from her, he pulled back. "I'm happy to walk with you. I'm enjoying my time and don't want to cut it short, just because of a few extra steps."

Emy cleared her throat.

"Um. Well. I thought I'd—we'd grab some coffee before walking over to the Champs-Élysées. It's a beautiful walk, and by the time we get over there, the lights should be turning on."

They stood on the cobblestones, daring to see who would move away first. Neither of them wanted the moment to end.

The day was catching up with them. Although unspoken, both of them started feeling the effects of the jetlag. Regardless, they were determined to stretch out the day as long as possible. As much as she wanted to stay in the moment, she knew they needed caffeine. And to start walking, or they might not last much longer.

"Okay. We can stand here and make out, or we can get going." Emy smiled up at him. His golden brown eyes smiled back at her as they started toward the Avenue of the Champs-Élysées.

"As much as I want to stand here and continue kissing you, we have places to be." They had been stealing kisses all day. She hoped that their last kiss wouldn't be *the* last kiss.

Emy and Jackson walked up to the first coffee stand they saw as they approached the Champs-Élysées. Jackson ordered two espressos and handed one to Emy.

"Can I ask you something?" she inquired curiously.

They had espressos in hand and were walking past the grand Dior store. Emy stopped to admire the store's holiday decor.

"Anything," he replied.

Emy wasn't someone who pried into other people's business. But she had spent the day kissing this man and really wanted to know more about him.

"How old are you, and why are you still single?" she blurted out awkwardly.

"That was two questions. And who said I was single?"

Emy gasped.

He nudged her jokingly. "Thirty-six, and I wish I knew why I'm still single. I've dated. I think it's hard to meet the right person, especially in the city."

Jackson finished his coffee. "I've been in several relationships over the years. Nothing has really worked out as I had hoped. Dating is exhausting. I'd rather put my energy elsewhere.

"What about you?" He tossed his cup into a trash bin to free up his hand.

"I'm thirty-three and perpetually single." Emy sighed. "Partly because my job keeps me away. Partly because I've dated almost everyone in New York. And when I say dated, I mean I've gone on a gazillion first dates that went nowhere. Being away from home means it's easier for me to get out of dating. It's hard out there for sure."

Emy's eyes were a mesmerizing shade of green. Her gaze could make anyone feel important, and her smile was infectious.

"I find it hard to believe you have a hard time dating. I can't imagine anyone not wanting to be with you."

Emy had flashbacks to her most recent dates and cringed. She wondered how she would convince him to go on a date with her when they returned home.

"My turn. Have you ever dated a passenger before?" probing into her dating habits.

"Once. And I may have flirted a time or two. But, I decided I would never cross that line again. I also dated a pilot before, but I learned quickly when that didn't end well either. Passengers and pilots are strictly off limits now."

Emy stopped and gave him a serious look. "You know, they could be serial killers!"

"Is that what you told your crew? That I was a serial killer?" Jackson laughed.

"No, I never said that. I told them you *could* be a serial killer. That's why Chloe shouldn't have given you my phone number. They convinced me otherwise."

Emy kept pace with Jackson as they approached the hotel.

The sun was just starting to set. But crowds still roamed the streets. "It's nice to see so many people out tonight." She held his hand as they walked.

Jackson paused in front of a building. He looked up. The historical architecture blended well with modern artistic elements, creating an inviting and inspiring space that mirrored Paris's dynamic art scene.

"This is the gallery I'll be working at for the next few days."

She could see Jackson's passion for art as he explained why he was there, and what he'd be doing, and this excited her. Each member of the Riley family had a hand in the family gallery.

"My older sisters are taking a less active role. It's mostly my sister, Jessica, and me that travel the most now," Jackson explained.

Working in the Paris gallery was apparently a regular occurrence for Jackson. "If it hadn't been for the timing, I would have been excited to make my way back to Paris. But with the holiday, it really complicated things for me. I really wanted to be with my family."

Knowing now how Jackson felt, Emy was relieved to be able to spend the day with him. She couldn't imagine how different things would have been to spend this day alone.

16

Jackson

Somehow, Emy and Jackson were back in front of the hotel faster than he would have liked. The day had gone by so quickly. He was tired, but wouldn't admit it. He didn't want their time together to end. It was almost 6:00 p.m.

Still hand in hand, they walked into the lobby together. Not sure of how to bring his time with Emy to an end, he turned to her. Just before he could say anything, Chloe bounced out of a chair in the lobby corner.

"Well, there you two are! I've been waiting for you two to return. I've been following you on Find My Friends all day, so I knew you were almost here. Isn't technology great? I didn't have to worry when you were coming back. If you stopped moving, I just checked to see where you were. Cyber stalking at its best."

Chloe was obviously feeling much better. Emy gave her a side-eye.

"Hi there, Jackson, how was your day?" Chloe was full of herself. He picked up on that upon their first meeting earlier in the day.

He could sense Emy pulling away to give him a little space.

"I hope you two are hungry. I called the restaurant and added a third person to our dinner reservation at 6:30, so we should get going."

Emy immediately turned to face Jackson. "You don't have to come with us if you don't want to. I know it's been a long day."

He didn't want to part ways with Emy. And Chloe had obviously taken the lead in ensuring their day continued.

Jackson wasn't going to let this opportunity vanish. For as long as he could remember, he had taken the easy way out. He had just spent an incredible day with this woman. Even though he was exhausted, he wasn't going to let it end now.

"Nope. I'm starving. Lead the way."

As he walked right over to Emy, her eyes widened. He took her hand as they followed Chloe out the door. After the three of them passed through the revolving door, Jackson caught a glimpse of Chloe. She smirked and shot Jackson a quick wink. Chloe was obviously on board with the two of them spending more time together.

He noticed Emy was quiet for the first time today. He and Chloe filled the blank space with talk about Paris, New York, and stories of trouble the girls used to get into. Chloe told stories from their early days as new-hire flight attendants. Emy let out a deep sigh of exhaustion. Jackson gave her hand an encouraging squeeze, and they continued walking to dinner.

"So, Chloe," Jackson began, "what should I know about Emy that I don't already know?"

He could tell Emy was nervous that her worlds were colliding. He tried his best to ensure she was comfortable. As she had mentioned earlier, it wasn't like her to kiss strangers, let alone a passenger from one of her flights.

They crossed over the street, turned a corner, and crossed the Pont des Art bridge. Before turning away from the Seine into the Latin Quarter, they paused for a minute to take in the view of Notre-Dame. Everyone chatted with ease. Chloe walked a bit faster, just ahead of Jackson and Emy, giving them a moment of privacy.

Jackson was still holding Emy's hand. He was relieved that she hadn't pulled away. He wanted to touch her. Holding her hand today, kissing her—so much of that was out of character for him. Jackson was normally reserved, which might have contributed to him meeting fewer people.

"Oh, here's something you should know about Emy—she loves desserts. Any dessert actually. It doesn't matter where we are; she's going to order dessert. But not just one. She always orders two. Not because she wants to try different desserts. Oh no, it's because she doesn't share."

Chloe turned and poked Emy in the shoulder. "Emy does. Not. Share. Dessert. Kinda like Joey from *Friends*, who doesn't share his food. That's our girl, Emy." Chloe laughed.

He could sense Emy hated being talked about. She didn't seem to like this revelation.

"That's so not true. I always share."

"Where's the lie, Emy?" Chloe squealed, nudging Emy.

"What? I order two for friends who say they don't eat dessert, but then expect me to share mine."

Just twenty-four hours ago, he was agitated and angry at his parents for sending him over to Paris on Christmas Eve. But right now, he couldn't wait to share dessert with this woman with the infectious laugh and made him smile. Something he had been missing in his life without even knowing it.

17

Emy

THE RESTAURANT WAS FULL OF YOUNG PEOPLE WHO HAD GATHERED TO CELEBRATE CHRISTMAS NIGHT. The lights were lit, the wine flowed, and conversations buzzed all around them. As Jackson, Emy, and Chloe talked, it was like they had been friends forever.

Occasionally, Emy found herself staring at Jackson. Was this really happening? Was she really here in Paris having dinner with someone she just met and her best friend? She accepted being cautiously happy.

Emy had never traveled with a companion before, other than Chloe. She never dated anyone long enough to want to travel with them, even though her benefits enabled her to travel for free, to just about anywhere in the world. She could tell pretty quickly if she wanted to pursue a relationship. And so far, she hadn't been inclined to continue anything.

Today seemed surreal. It was almost like they were working backward. What would it be like when they were back in New York?

Chloe filled their glasses with wine. The dishes had long been cleared, and now they were waiting on the desserts they had ordered.

Emy could tell Chloe had been watching both of them all night. Even though Emy was exhausted, she could still pick up on what Chloe was thinking. It wasn't often that Chloe got to see Emy interact with a potential new love interest. It had been so long since she had connected with anyone. Knowing these moments were rare, neither of them wanted to rush the evening.

As their server set down a plate of assorted French macarons and a crème brûlée, all eyes shifted to Emy. She pulled the crème brûlée closer, then pushed the plate of macarons toward Chloe and Jackson as her way of telling them where they stood with the dessert options.

He picked up a spoon and moved closer to Emy and her dessert. As he took a big scoop of the crème brûlée, she stared at him. Just before the spoonful entered his mouth, he admitted, "Crème brûlée is my favorite dessert!"

Emy couldn't look away. Jackson set his spoon down on the side of the plate and turned his attention back to Chloe. This left Emy lingering over her dessert. Apparently, crème brûlée was now her favorite too.

"Jackson, how long are you in Paris?" Chloe asked.

"I'm not actually sure, to be honest. We have a February show coming up in our gallery. Each item needs to be cataloged and shipped. I was sent over to make sure everything worked out. I'll be at the gallery tomorrow morning. After some time there, I'll have a better idea. If all goes well, I'm hoping to be back before the New Year."

Emy was curious about his New Year's plans and who he'd be spending it with. He quickly put her at ease. "I have a standing date with four beautiful girls. They all might be under ten, but we can really shake things up."

The three of them laughed, and Jackson filled them in on the New Year's Eve tradition with his nieces.

Emy watched him closely as he talked about his nieces. She leaned in on her elbows, listening intently as he described what it was like being with them.

"We stay up as late as we can and pop the cork on some sparkling cider while wearing our crowns. No better way to ring in the New Year." Jackson then raised his glass to Emy and Chloe. "Thank you both for including me in your Christmas plans. I truly had a great day. Cheers."

Emy noticed his gaze lingered on her. Her head was spinning, but it wasn't from the wine.

"That tradition sounds fabulous!"

Emy started to tear up. How had she gone so many years alone? She realized she wanted to be with Jackson on New Year's Eve; she wanted to wear a crown with him.

Chloe cleared her throat. Emy was fading. It was a combination of the wine, lack of sleep, and an overload of emotions. Emy was already fragile going into the trip, and was beating herself up over her single life.

"It's a good thing we get to spend New Year's with 300 of our best friends. Right, Emy?" Emy could tell Chloe was trying to pull her out of a funk before Jackson noticed.

"Well, one of us will be. You'll be home this year. Much deserved." Emy stood up, letting everyone know she was done with dinner.

She didn't want Jackson to see her falling apart.

"I'm excited that you get to spend New Year's with Patrick. He's a lucky man. You two deserve to be together."

Jackson wasn't moving. "You'll be flying on New Year's?"

She had seen that look over and over again. As soon as a guy found out she'd be working a holiday, or she couldn't spontaneously leave for the weekend, things were over before they started.

"Yes, I always try to swap out holiday trips so families can stay together." Emy wrapped her scarf around her neck and gave Jackson a head tilt. "We need to get back. We have an early pick-up in the morning."

The air was thick as reality set in. Emy knew she had just changed the vibe. Today was no different than any other date. She had an amazing day with Jackson, and now it was coming to an end.

"Are we ready? I got us a cab. I figured it was getting too cold to walk back." Chloe had been outside and missed the exchange with Jackson. It wasn't worth reliving, so Emy perked up for the sake of the ride back to the hotel.

As they were walking out, Jackson wrapped his arm around Emy's shoulders, shielding her from the cold and helping her into the cab. She knew the ride back would be quick and wanted to hold on to the next few minutes just a little bit longer.

18

Jackson

JACKSON WASN'T SURE WHAT HE WAS EXPECTING, BUT HE HAD IT IN HIS HEAD THAT HE WANTED TO SPEND NEW YEAR'S EVE WITH EMY. Sadly, she'd be working. He understood now why she had looked at him the way she had back at the restaurant. She had probably assumed he was like others she had dated before. The ones that bailed before things got started.

But he hadn't felt this way in a long time. This would not be the end. Not by a long shot.

As they pulled up to the Hôtel du Louvre, Chloe gave them a quick hug and kiss on both cheeks.

"It was nice to meet you, Jackson. I hope this isn't the last time I'll be seeing you."

"I feel the same, Chloe. If it's up to me, I'll see you again sooner than later." Jackson returned a wink to Chloe as she started toward the steps of the hotel.

Before she walked away, Chloe turned back to Emy. "Hey. Take your time. See where this is going. You deserve to be happy, Emy. It's okay to live a little."

She gave Emy a loud kiss on the cheek and ran up the stairs to the door.

Emy and Jackson stood still in the cold air outside. He took the first step, moving closer and closer until he leaned down and touched his nose to hers. She smiled.

"Emy, thank you for the best first date I've ever had."

Before she could say anything, Jackson kissed the tip of her nose and walked her into the hotel lobby.

He had Emy's hand in his. He walked over to the elevator and didn't let go. They each pushed the buttons to their respective floors. They rode up to his floor and stopped, and when the door opened, he turned to her.

"I'd like you to come with me. I know you need to be up early in the morning, but I'm not ready for this to end."

"I'm not ready for it to end either." She stepped out of the elevator with him.

They walked to his room, still hand in hand. Jackson opened the door and led Emy into his room. The door gently closed behind them.

19

Emy

EMY REALIZED SHE WAS ALONE WITH JACKSON. It wasn't like her to move so quickly. She heard Chloe in her head telling her it was her time. Her heart began to beat harder in her chest. She turned to face him as he closed the distance between them. She was no longer cold as the heat between them warmed her to the core.

Jackson skimmed her lower lip with his thumb before he leaned in and kissed her gently. As their lips moved together, she let out a soft moan. He parted from her lips and rested his forehead on hers.

"Emy, tell me if you want me to stop," he said quietly in her ear.

She tried to speak, barely able to whisper.

"I don't want you to stop, Jackson."

Even though she had spent the day with him stealing kisses, this was different. It was as though they both needed this. It had been so long since she had been with someone. And even though she had just met Jackson, she had never felt so wanted before. He took her hand and led her further into the room.

Emy had felt a connection the moment she saw him. But now it was more than just a physical need. She let Jackson continue to kiss her. With each kiss, their desire grew. He stopped and looked down at her.

"Open your eyes, Emy. I want you."

She couldn't look away; instead, she started to remove his clothes. She pulled his scarf away from his coat, dropping it to the floor next to where they stood. She had to lift up onto her toes to get his coat down from his broad shoulders. Then she tossed it on the chair in the corner.

Sliding her arms around his neck, she moved her body into his, kissing him like she had never kissed anyone before.

He untied her coat, tossing it aside. He reached under her sweater and slipped it over her head. Emy's breath quickened as she stood before him in just her bra. Within seconds, they were exploring each other's bodies as their clothing fell away.

Jackson's hands slid up her sides and found their way to her breasts.

"Emy, you are exquisite" he said between kissing her neck, making his way down to her breasts. He unhooked the back of her bra, pulling it down, leaving her soft breasts exposed. She shivered as he circled her bare nipple with his tongue.

With each stroke, Emy felt more alive than ever before. She tried to pull him to her, but Jackson slid down to the floor in front of her.

"Jackson?" She tried to speak but couldn't.

He began unbuttoning her jeans and pulled them down over her hips and off each leg, tossing them, along with her panties. Emy closed her eyes and laid back as he explored the path leading him between her legs. He started kissing her stomach moving down to her navel.

Her creamy skin glistened in the moonlight. She shuddered as he licked her inner thighs and moved to her inner folds. Arching her back, she grabbed the top of his hair as he entered her with his tongue. She was already surrendering to Jackson completely when he slipped his fingers between her legs. Just when she didn't think she could last much longer, Emy cried out.

He slowly made his way up onto the bed, hovering over Emy. Her breath was rapid and shallow. As Jackson's mouth met hers, she could feel his arousal between her legs as he slid up her body, joining her.

He continued to find her breasts, licking each nipple. She couldn't catch her breath, still trying to recover from the last climax, her arms circling his bare back. She could feel every muscle in his lean body.

Before Jackson positioned himself between her legs, he reached over to his overnight bag, fumbling through until he found what he was looking for. As he rolled on a condom, he never looked away from Emy.

Pausing for just a brief minute, Jackson found his way back to her mouth.

Emy's breath quickened as he moved deep inside her. There was an urgency emanating from both of them. He quickened his pace to match Emy's breath. He couldn't look away from her; he had never wanted anyone more.

She could feel every muscle tighten as Jackson moved over her.

"I'm not going to last much longer; I need you," she cried as she trembled beneath him.

Jackson didn't have time to say anything as he climaxed, then collapsed onto her.

"Are you okay?" He had propped himself on one elbow, looking down at her. He moved a strand of hair away from her face to get a better look into her eyes.

Reaching up to stroke his arm, she whispered, "I've never been better." She closed her eyes and fell into a deep sleep.

20

Jackson

JACKSON SPENT THE BETTER PART OF THE NIGHT WATCHING EMY SLEEP. He had never been a one-night-stand kind of guy. He felt something for her he had never felt before.

He reached over, caressing her hair. Her milky complexion shone in from what was left of the moonlight, shining in from the window. He wasn't sure how he would say goodbye in just a few short hours. But if it was up to him, this was only the beginning.

Emy roused, barely awake but conscious of Jackson's presence. As if she knew what he was thinking, She reached out and pulled him close to her. He breathed in her hair; she smelled so good. He started to feel heat making its way through his body, and he could no longer control his erection.

This time, he felt a desire for more than just sex. He wanted to unite with Emy. Everything she was, he wanted it all.

With her eyes still closed, she reached down and held Jackson's erection in her hand. He groaned.

He started to kiss her again; he couldn't get enough of her. In just a few hours, she'd be on her way back to New York. He needed to feel her one more time. "If you keep touching me like that, I'm not going to last much longer."

He moved his hand between her legs. Her thighs spread apart, and she rocked her hips to meet Jackson's rhythm. Emy rolled on top of him, taking control. This time, she took pleasure in rolling the condom on his fully erect penis. She looked deep into his eyes and slid Jackson inside her.

The two of them found a rapid pace, matching each other, move for move. Before long, Emy collapsed in his arms. Both of them were breathing hard, wrapped in each other's arms.

Morning was just a couple hours away. They had to get some sleep.

21

Emy

IT FELT LIKE THEY HAD ONLY BEEN ASLEEP FOR A FEW MINUTES BEFORE EMY'S ALARM STARTED TO GO OFF. She reached for her phone to silence the alarm, trying not to wake Jackson. She slowly climbed out of the bed when he started to stir.

Emy whispered, "Sorry, I was trying not to wake you." She gathered her clothes from the floor.

"You didn't think you were going to sneak out without saying anything, did you?"

Jackson sat up and ran his hand through his hair. He grabbed his boxers from the floor, slipped them on, and walked toward Emy.

She pulled on the layer of clothes they had peeled off just a few hours before. She needed to move fast because she had to be in the lobby in just over an hour.

"Jackson. I don't know what this is…"

But before she could say anything else, he was closing in and staring down at her.

"I don't either, but I want to find out." He took her hand and kissed her palm. "This was more than just a great time for me. I know you have to go, but I want to see you again. Sooner than later."

He let go of her hand and sat down on the edge of the bed to let her finish getting dressed.

"Me too," Emy said quietly, tears building behind her lashes.

She was relieved that this would not be it. Picking up her phone, she smiled.

"Shoot, my phone is dead; I really have to go."

She looked around her, making sure she had everything before she said goodbye.

Jackson reached over and grabbed his coat off the chair. He reached inside the pocket and pulled out the Infinite Airlines cocktail napkin with "Emerson Nichols" and her phone number written on it.

"Is this really your number?" he asked with an inquisitive smirk on his face.

She laughed. "Yes, yes, it is. It looks like Chloe saved us after all."

Emy jumped up and grabbed her coat and scarf. She headed toward the door but paused just before she opened it. She turned and walked back to the bed where he was still waiting, cupped his face in her hands, and gently kissed him.

"Would you have called me if we hadn't run into each other?"

He stared at her for a moment.

"I don't know. I know now that I would have regretted it every single day if I hadn't." Jackson leaned in and kissed her gently.

"I'll call you before your flight departs for New York."

She left Jackson's room feeling hopeful for the first time in a long time. She had such a great time with him and looked forward to seeing him again back home. Now she had to scramble to charge her phone and get herself ready for the twelve-hour shift ahead of her.

✈

22

Jackson

JACKSON COULDN'T RETURN TO SLEEP AFTER EMY HAD LEFT, SO HE DECIDED TO TAKE A QUICK SHOWER. He already missed her and wished she was in the shower with him. It was crazy how much had changed since landing in Paris. He didn't know he could miss someone so much after just meeting them. But she had changed his entire perspective. He hoped she felt the same and couldn't wait to message her.

He had a couple of hours before his first meeting at 10:00 a.m. That gave him just enough time to grab some coffee and shoot her a quick message before he needed to start working. He almost forgot why he was in Paris. And now, he just wanted to be back home in New York.

As Jackson exited the hotel, he headed directly to Café de la Tartine. This time, he'd be sitting alone. With hands in his pocket, he clung to the napkin with Emy's phone number. He was glad he had verified that the number was in fact hers. With a smile, he walked into the café. He sat down at a table against the window and placed his order quickly, eager to send his first text to her.

Settling into his space, he pulled his phone out of one pocket and the napkin out of the other. Just as he was about to enter her phone number, the barista clumsily lowered a fresh cup of coffee, accidentally knocking the cup over the saucer in the process. He tried to grab the napkin, but not before the dark espresso encompassed the entire Infinite Airlines logo *and* the phone number.

"Jesus! *No!*"

He jumped up to avoid the hot liquid. Before he was able to salvage the napkin, the server instinctively swept the table with her rag, apologizing as she continued to sweep the table.

Jackson could see the napkin crumble and break apart in the process. Grabbing the napkin out of the barista's rag, he did his best to shake off the dark liquid and salvage any remnants of Emy's number. There was nothing left to salvage. The napkin, along with the phone number inscribed on it, was unrecognizable.

"Mes excuses, monsieur." The barista apologized to Jackson again.

It wasn't her fault that Jackson's only connection to Emy had just disintegrated before his eyes.

"Damn it!"

Jackson ran his hand over his face, unsure what to do. He grabbed his jacket off the back of the chair and hurried out the café door. If he was quick enough, he might be able to catch the crew shuttle before they left for the airport.

Café de la Tartine was just a few blocks away. But as he ran down the cobblestone street, it felt like miles. He had to get there before they left. He leaped up the steps leading up to the door and arrived at the front desk completely out of breath.

As sweat dripped off his brow, his stuttered words spilled out in bursts between rapid breaths.

"Hi, can you please… tell me if the Infinite flight crew… has left yet? My friend is a flight attendant… and I forgot to give her… something to take back home."

The young girl working the desk said, "I'm sorry, sir, but I'm not allowed to give you that information. However, I did see you with your friend earlier. She left just over an hour ago."

Jackson groaned in despair and put his head down on the desk. His meeting was in thirty minutes, but he absolutely had to try to reach Emy. There was no way she could leave Paris before he got to her.

He had to get to the airport immediately. Jackson pulled out his phone and ordered an Uber, then called his good friend at the gallery, Colleen, to let her know something had come up.

He felt physically sick, realizing he had no way of reaching Emy ever again.

23

Emy

EMY ENTERED HER ROOM WITH LESS THAN AN HOUR TO SPARE. She plugged in her phone to charge before jumping in the shower. Her head was spinning from the hours spent in Paris. She wished she could call Jackson to tell him what an amazing time she'd had, how she never could have predicted meeting him. What was supposed to be a girls' overnight trip to Paris ended up being something very different.

Just as she was about to dry her hair, there was a loud knock on her door. With a smile on her face, she opened the door.

Chloe stood on the other side of the door with a coffee in hand, shoving it toward Emy.

"Well, well, well. Judging by that smile you initially had on your face, and the frown that is crossing it now, I am guessing you were hoping for someone else."

Chloe held a pan au chocolate in her hand and pushed past Emy into the hotel room as she took a bite.

"Come on in," Emy said flatly as she let the door close and walked back into the bathroom, turning on the hair dryer.

Chloe followed her into the small space and sat down on the closed toilet seat, waiting for Emy to share the details of her evening with Jackson.

She turned to Chloe. "I don't kiss and tell."

Chloe let out a robust laugh.

"Liar! Emy, we've been roommates for the last ten years. I know everything about you. Spill it. And don't leave anything out. I want all the details."

Emy filled Chloe in from the time they came back to the hotel. As she told her the details, Chloe stood up and hugged her.

"I don't think I have seen you this happy in so long, Emy. I am so proud of you for putting yourself first for once."

Emy was finishing up the final touches on her makeup when Chloe asked, "So, what's next? How did you guys leave things?"

"In a hurry," Emy responded nervously. "I didn't have much time, and my phone was dead. Thankfully you had already given him my number, and he asked if it was real just before I left."

Both girls were still chuckling as they pulled their roller bags into the hallway and set off down to the lobby to meet the rest of the crew.

"I guess I owe you one. But no more passing out my number to strangers."

As they walked through the lobby, Emy looked around in hopes of seeing Jackson one last time. It was still early; he had probably gone back to bed. It was still a few hours before her flight departed. She couldn't wait to hear from him again.

"Uh-oh," Chloe teased as they made their way out to the shuttle bus. "I know that look. That's the 'Emy's in love' look!"

Emy elbowed her to keep her quiet, but not before the entire group heard.

Jeff was mid-sentence when the girls climbed in the shuttle and settled into their seats. Allen leaned over the back of their seats. "I can't wait for this one. Things just got very interesting."

Emy turned five shades of red. She pulled out her sunglasses and slid them over her eyes.

"I have no idea what any of you are talking about."

Emy looked out the window. She glanced at her phone, checking for a missed text or call.

Since when did I become the girl waiting by the phone?

When I became the girl who slept with a complete stranger after spending a day with him.

As the shuttle pulled away from their hotel, Emy wondered if she should rethink her life choices.

24

Jackson

JACKSON HAD NO IDEA WHAT HE WOULD DO ONCE HE GOT THERE. It took almost an hour to get to Charles de Gaulle airport. He had just over an hour before Emy's flight departed.

His Uber pulled up to the curb. For the second time that day, he bolted out and ran as if his life depended on it. When he arrived at the Infinite Airlines ticket counter, he knew his options were limited.

"Can I please get a message to Emerson Nichols on the Infinite flight to JFK?"

He knew this sounded crazy, but he had everything to lose at this point. He filled the agent in on why he needed to get a message to her, and he deposited the wadded-up ball of a napkin that once had Emy's number written on it onto the ticket counter for the agent to see.

"I'm sorry, sir. There are only a few of us working, and it looks like that JFK flight is already boarding. There's no way we can get to the gate, but let me try to call."

The agent picked up the phone and tried calling the gate. Jackson stood impatiently at the desk, trying to hold it together.

"Unfortunately, they must be busy boarding. If you want to step aside, I can try to call again in a minute."

Panic started to set in.

"Could I buy a ticket for that flight?"

He was not about to lose his chance with Emy. Getting on that flight seemed like a logical solution.

"Sir, they have already started the boarding process; you would never make it. And the system won't let me sell you a ticket with less than an hour before the departure."

The agent gave Jackson a sympathetic look.

"What if I bought a ticket to somewhere else? I don't care where. Somewhere that would let me get through security. I just need to get a message to her before she takes off; I won't actually go anywhere."

Jackson knew he sounded crazy and wondered if the agent would call security on him.

The agent typed as fast as she could, trying to find another available flight that would allow him to get through security. She obviously took pity on him.

"Here, there's a flight close to the JFK flight, but you'll have to hurry. I'll just need your credit card and passport."

Jackson threw his hands in the air, rocking back on his heels. His passport was back at the hotel. There was no way he would get to Emy. A message to the gate seemed impossible.

As he took a breath, reality settled in. There wasn't much else he could do.

25

Emy

THE GATE AGENT WORKING EMY'S FLIGHT HEARD THE PHONE RINGING BUT COULDN'T MAKE IT IN TIME TO ANSWER THE PHONE. The team was short-handed, and she was doing her best to get the flight out on time. Emy watched the agent hurry down the jet bridge with final paperwork, then hand it to her.

"Have a great flight," the agent said and helped Emy close the main cabin door for departure.

"Ladies and gentlemen, at this time, all cellular phones and electronic devices must be turned off and stored. Before the airplane leaves the gate, you must be seated with your seat belt fastened, your tray table and footrest stored, and your baggage secured."

Emy handed off the paperwork to the cockpit before heading back to join Allen in the back of the plane. Her phone was in her pocket, still turned on. She intended to switch it into airplane mode when she got to her jumpseat.

She was working with Allen, and he could sense she was putting on a good face for the sake of their passengers.

"Nothing yet?"

He closed up the last of the carts that had been loaded onto the plane by catering services.

She shook her head, pulling her phone out one last time before taking her seat.

From the front of the cabin, Chloe caught a glimpse of Emy. She could tell from her face that Emy hadn't heard from Jackson. This would be a very long flight if a call or text didn't come through in the next few minutes.

Emy opened the phone to her photos and found the selfie she had taken with Jackson in front of the Flame of Liberty. She pushed back a tear starting to form. There was no way she would cry over someone she had just met.

As she felt the plane lifting off, Emy took one last look at her phone before activating airplane mode. She was in the very back of the airplane with Allen. She looked over at him sitting in the jumpseat across the galley.

"It's going to be okay, kid." He gave her a wink.

She tried to smile back but couldn't. How could she have been so wrong about Jackson? How did she let herself get so worked up in thinking he could be the one for her?

As the plane reached 10,000 feet, Emy and Allen got up out of their seats to start setting up the beverage carts. He closed the galley curtains for privacy.

Emy was quiet. In her early years of flying, she made several dating mistakes and thought she had learned from them. Since then, she vowed to never date another passenger or pilot again. She broke her number one rule. The thought of meeting someone on a flight had not crossed her mind since.

Maybe it was the thought of Chloe about to get married, leaving her alone that she had given in and let her guard down. *No dating passengers, Emy!*

But this was far worse. She had seen a future with Jackson. They talked about what they'd be doing in New York, meeting family and friends. This was a huge blow.

Allen could see the road Emy was on and knew she needed an intervention. Judging by the look on her face, if he didn't do something now, it would be too late.

"Hey. Let's talk about it. I know you. We've been flying together a long time. You can talk to me."

He grabbed Emy's hand that had just put an ice bucket on the top of the cart.

She held it for a few seconds, feeling hot tears building up behind her lashes.

"I'll be fine. I just made a stupid mistake. I can't believe I spent an entire day with him. And I'm sure you can guess that I also spent the night."

Emy groaned as she started piling cups on top of the cart.

"I'm just so angry at myself."

Emy knew she needed to put it aside for now. She couldn't cry her way down the aisle while serving drinks, for Christ's sake.

"Can I ask you something?" Allen moved around the galley on autopilot, loading coffee, cups, and ice on top of the second cart. "Did he seem to have a good time?"

Emy leaned back against the galley counter, putting her hands over her face. She took a deep breath before she looked back at Allen.

"I had an amazing time. He seemed to have a good time too. He even gave me an out. That's why it stings so badly. I would never have stayed the night with him had I thought otherwise. He just seemed so together, no nonsense. We'd both got to this point in our lives from not playing games like most people do."

Allen speculated, "I'm betting you'll have a call waiting for you on the other side of the pond. Trust me, I didn't pick up prick vibes from him. We have been doing this long enough to know when someone is a jerk or not. Plus, you're a really good judge of character. This doesn't sound like a one-nighter for either of you. So, before we implode, let's give this guy the benefit of the doubt. Maybe you rocked his world and he overslept."

They both laughed off the emotions. She stepped into the lavatory to check her makeup, blow her nose, and take a deep breath before they made their way into the aisles to start the first of three beverage services of the day.

∞

THEY WERE SEVERAL HOURS INTO THE FLIGHT BEFORE CHLOE GOT A CHANCE TO RETURN TO THE BACK OF THE PLANE. Chloe picked up the phone and made the crew rest break announcement in both English and French.

"*Ladies and Gentlemen. We have completed our inflight lunch service. Due to the length of this flight, Pilots and Flight Attendants will be taking a rest break. Be assured a complete crew is on duty at all times in the cockpit and in the cabins to assist you.*"

After she hung up the phone, Chloe secured the curtain into place so they could finally catch up.

"Finally. How are we doing back here?" Chloe looked to Allen, who gave her a confirming nod. As she cleaned up the galley, Emy poured herself a ginger ale.

"Oh no, that bad? I haven't seen you drink that in years."

Chloe walked over and grabbed a cup and ice and poured the rest of Emy's can into another cup.

"I'm fine. Really. It was stupid of me to get carried away." Emy leaned against the counter, trying not to think about it. "You should be asking Allen how he's doing. He's the one who's suffering back here with me."

Chloe stood next to Emy. "I feel horrible. This is all my fault. None of this would have happened if I hadn't pushed so hard. I'm really sorry, Emy. We both spent time with him; I would never have pegged him for a ghoster."

"Seriously, Chloe. I've been through a lot worse. Please don't make a big deal of this. The only reason we're even still talking about it now is we have nothing else to talk about for another five hours. If we were already home, we would laugh about it and move on."

Emy wasn't sure if she was trying to convince her friends or herself. Either way, she wasn't buying her own consoling. But for their sake, she'd try her best to put on a smile and get through the rest of the flight.

A passenger call light came on.

"I've got it." Emy went to check on what they needed.

Chloe turned to Allen. "How bad is it?'

"Bad. She's putting on a brave face, but I think this one is going to be hard to get over if he doesn't message her."

Allen poured himself coffee into a cup, noting that he definitely preferred working first class instead of this.

✈

26

Jackson

JACKSON FELT PHYSICALLY SICK, AND THE RIDE BACK TO THE HOTEL WASN'T HELPING. Nothing he came up with made sense. And worst yet, he had to go to work. The gallery needed him, and he was on a timeline to get things done.

The knot in his stomach only worsened as he realized he still didn't have a return flight back home. He was stuck and couldn't find a solution. It was the middle of the night back in New York, so there wasn't much he could do now even if he wanted to.

He rode directly to the gallery where he'd spend the next few days getting everything prepared for the loan shipment. He would oversee the packing, protection, and transport of the borrowed art. Since this was a private collection, the artist was eager to lend the work to the Riley family gallery. Until he could figure out a plan on how to reach Emy, he had to find a way to focus on the art.

∞

"IT'S SO GOOD TO SEE YOU, JACKSON! We're really excited to show this work in the States."

Colleen was the art director at the gallery and had worked with Jackson's family for many years. She had known Jackson since he was just a boy.

Colleen knew he was always pleasing at least one of his four sisters. He loved each one dearly and would do anything for any of them. Even if they gave him a hard time.

"How are the women in your life these days? Still giving you a hard time?"

"You know how those women are." Jackson winked at her.

Colleen couldn't understand how he was still single. He was charming, and she enjoyed her time with him. She was excited for Jackson to meet the new artist, Lucy. Colleen couldn't wait to see the chemistry between them.

"Lucy should be here any minute. While we wait, let me show you the pieces you'll be taking back with you."

Colleen was like a second mother to Jackson. She was easy to work with, and her passion for the arts was undeniable. She had a soft spot for Jackson and felt sorry for him, knowing how his sisters gave him such a hard time. He took his responsibility and position in the family like a champ.

His love of art was deeply ingrained and traced its roots back to his family's legacy. The family gallery became a sanctuary of inspiration. A place where he could witness the transformative power of art firsthand. It was there that Jackson developed a profound appreciation for so many diverse forms of artistic expression.

Working in the family business provided him with the opportunity to not only preserve and showcase the artistic treasures passed down through generations but also to contribute to the ongoing narrative of the art world. The gallery became more than just a repository of artifacts; it became a living testament to the passion and dedication that fueled his love for art.

Through his work, he found purpose in curating exhibitions, organizing events, and sharing the beauty of art with the world. The family gallery became a canvas on which Jackson painted his own chapter. A labor of love that connected him to his heritage and allowed him to contribute to the cultural enrichment of others. It also allowed him the freedom to travel. But like Emy, he was starting to wonder if he had traveled the right path.

Lucy arrived just after 11:00 a.m. As she stepped into the gallery halls, an air of effortless grace enveloped her.

Dressed in a curated ensemble that seamlessly married bohemian flair with Parisian chic, she moved with a captivating rhythm. The soft sway of her artistically layered garments mirrored the brushstrokes of her own creations. Her steps, purposeful yet unhurried, conveyed a quiet confidence, and the click-clack of her heeled boots against the polished museum floor added extra flair to her entrance.

Any other time in his life, Jackson would have immediately been curious about someone like Lucy. She was beautiful, smart, and enchanting for sure. Though her beauty was undeniable, his interest was firmly rooted in the enchantment of her artistry and nothing more.

This thought brought him right back around to Emy. If he hadn't already figured it out before, he knew now that she was the one for him.

Jackson did his best to ensure he gave his client the best attention he could. But his focus was to get this job done as quickly as possible and then get home. He knew he'd have a better chance of finding Emy once he was back in New York.

"I think we have everything we need. Lucy. It's a pleasure working with you. I'm sure your art will show quite well in our gallery."

He was short but professional. He noticed Colleen giving him a slight head tilt. Had she picked up on his desire to wrap up quickly?

"Yes. Thank you. I'm very excited as well. I plan to come over in the coming weeks. Maybe while you're in town, we can get coffee and you can share your thoughts with me." Lucy was putting her coat back on to leave. "How long are you here in Paris?"

"I'm hoping to wrap up as quickly as possible. Something came up at home, and I'd like to get back as soon as possible."

Jackson tried to avoid Colleen's curious gaze. The last thing he needed was his family finding out about Emy and a rushed job in Paris. They counted on him, and he didn't want to let them down.

He had to find Emy.

Once Lucy had left the building, Colleen turned to Jackson.

"That's not how I thought that was going to go." She crossed her arms and tapped her foot. "What's going on, monsieur?"

27

Emy

What was supposed to be the best trip at the start had turned into a pity party at best. Emy tried her best to shake the sadness she felt, but she just couldn't pull herself out of it. Allen had flown with her for years and knew she was trying her best to put on a good face. He also hated seeing her hurting.

"Hey, kid, you're a catch. I've been saying it for years. Regardless of what happens next, you are one of a kind. Whatever happens doesn't define you."

Allen gave her a quick hug before they sat in their jump seats for landing. She was lucky to work with some of the best flight attendants at Infinite.

He was right—whatever happened, she was in good company, and she would not let this define her.

"Ladies and gentlemen, welcome to New York, JFK airport. Local time is 12:45 p.m."

Chloe finished the announcement from the front of the airplane as it taxied to the terminal. It was 6:45 p.m. in Paris. Emy was still strapped into her jumpseat, and her phone was still in her pocket in airplane mode.

As the plane taxied to the terminal, she decided not to check her phone until she was away from everyone. She had been so happy getting into the crew shuttle just hours ago. She didn't want to have to admit to anyone that Jackson hadn't called her.

Emy waited until the last of the passengers were out of the aisle and near the exit before she pulled out her phone. Then she turned airplane mode off and put her phone back in her pocket.

Retrieving her rollerboard from the overhead bin, she wheeled it toward the door. She could see Chloe waiting for her. Emy was exhausted and wanted to get home.

"Well?" Chloe stood in the jetway waiting for Emy to update her.

Chloe had prayed the whole flight that Jackson had come through. When they landed, there should be a text.

"I don't know. I'm afraid to look. I have several notifications, but I'm not sure any are from him."

Emy couldn't even say his name. She knew before she looked that he hadn't messaged her. They started up the jetway and said goodbyes to the rest of the crew.

"Emy, see you on New Year's Eve!" Allen shouted from behind them.

She had made sure she picked up a shift that also had her friends on it. It had almost become a tradition to work holidays with Allen and Jeff. They were her family in the sky. If things were not going well, she'd at least have them to comfort her.

Emy gave a quick wave, then winked at Allen.

"Wouldn't want it any other way!"

Emy had been excited to be on the trip with Allen and Jeff. But knowing she'd be flying back to Paris made her stomach feel sick.

Emy and Chloe were walking through the terminal when Chloe watched Emy pull out her phone. She scrolled for what seemed like forever before she looked over to Chloe, then shook her head.

The two walked in silence until they reached the exit. They'd take the train home, just as they did coming into work just a few days ago.

They were both off for the next five days and had plans to shop for Chloe's wedding dress. The task seemed daunting now, but there was no way Emy would ruin this time for her best friend.

As they walked to the train, Emy looked straight ahead.

"I know what you're thinking, and you need to stop. I am going to be fine." Emy reached over and took her friend's hand. "And you are in no way responsible for this. I am an adult; I make my own choices. If I didn't want to spend time with him, I wouldn't have. So don't beat yourself up over this."

Emy let go of her friend's hand, and she saw Chloe wipe a tear from her eye. They rode the rest of the way into the city in silence. Emy tried to be strong.

Chloe felt horrible for her friend, and that she was responsible for getting Emy involved with Jackson.

"Want me to stay the night tonight? We can have a sleepover like old times."

"Absolutely not! I'm not that fragile. Let's forget this ever happened, okay? We have a fun week ahead."

Just before their stop, Emy sat up straight, "Okay, where are we going this week?

She wasn't going to be a downer for Chloe. The two had talked about wedding dresses since the proposal and couldn't wait to shop at some of the best wedding boutiques in the city. It had taken Chloe months to get these appointments and there was no way they were going to miss it.

"Are you sure you still want to go?" Chloe doubted Emy would be up for shopping and didn't want to push her to a dark place.

"You're kidding me, right? You promised me free champagne and carte blanche on my maid-of-honor dress! I'm not missing this for anything." Emy gave Chloe a shove with her shoulder. "Do me a favor—let's not talk about this whole Jackson thing again, okay? I promise you, I'm going to be fine. I'll let you know if I need a shoulder to cry on. But for now, I'm going to be okay. We've been looking forward to this week for months. Nothing is going to spoil it."

They arrived at their stop. With no rain in sight, they came out of the station to bright blue skies. Emy walked to Chloe's apartment and parted ways with her, then moved on to her own West Village home. They made plans to meet up the next day to start dress shopping. Emy was looking forward to it.

She opened the door, and Marie was right there to greet her. She tossed her keys in a bowl on the sidebar as she stepped inside. Marie circled her feet, waiting to be acknowledged.

Emy paused at the mirror as she took off her scarf and coat. She stared at the woman looking back at her. It had been a long time since she felt this drained. She was exhausted and glad to be home.

She picked up Marie and walked over to her window.

"This, girl, is why I'm always gone. I like to avoid my reality. When did we become so pathetic?"

Setting Marie down, she grabbed her bag. She'd unpack and start to think about what she'd be doing for the next five days while home.

Maybe a roommate wasn't such a bad idea. If she opened her apartment to another flight attendant, she'd still have privacy. But maybe things wouldn't be so quiet.

The apartment felt cold, which didn't help the feelings she was having. She turned up the heat and started her unpacking routine. As she began to unpack, her phone rang. Her heart pounded in her chest. Was it him?

Disappointingly, she saw her mom's name on the caller ID. "Hey, mom."

Emy tried her best to smile. Just hearing her mom's voice on the other end made her tear up. Feeling like a teenager again, she told her mom about Jackson. Thankfully, she could have these talks with her mom. She didn't hold back and didn't spare any details from her Christmas trip.

"Oh, Emy. I wish I was with you. I can hear how sad you are. Relationships are complicated, and sometimes they don't go the way we hope. But you're strong, my love. You've always been resilient. Remember that."

"And I'd be lying to you if I didn't know firsthand what you're going through. It took me a few flights to figure out that passengers and pilots are not the best *dates*." Her mom laughed.

"And before you say it, I'm aware I married your dad. But it was a very different time then. And he's an exception for sure."

Emy loved her parents so much and missed them terribly. After she got off the phone with her mom, she made a mental note that she needed to visit them. They'd be passing through after the New Year, and she wanted to make sure she was home to see them.

28

Jackson

"SIT." Colleen motioned to the mid-century chairs at the front of the gallery. Jackson and Colleen were alone after Lucy left.

"I was hoping to play cupid this time around. Lucy is adorable and smart. I thought you'd connect with her. She's really, really great and just your type."

It was hard for him to sit still. For the last hour, he had been looking at his watch, trying to determine when Emy's flight would land. He planned to call home soon but knew he had to wait for at least another hour to do it. He just hoped he wasn't too late.

"I actually met someone," he admitted. "Her name is Emerson. She was the flight attendant on my flight to Paris. But long story short, I lost her number. She's been waiting for me to text her, but I couldn't."

Jackson hung his head low and stared at the floor. With his elbows resting on his knees, he rubbed his hands together as he told Colleen the entire story, including how he tried to buy a ticket for *any* flight, just to say goodbye and get her number again.

She didn't know what to say. She reached over and put her hand on his knee.

"Come. Let's find this Emerson Nichols."

Colleen scooted over to her computer. Since the gallery opened later that day, the two of them had it entirely to themselves.

A quick Google search led them down one rabbit hole after another. How could Emy not be on social media at all? She traveled, for Christ's sake. Once he found her, he'd have to commend her on her privacy strategy. But that wasn't helpful now.

"Wait, she had a friend with her; it was her roommate, Chloe."

Colleen typed in 'Chloe' along with 'Infinite Airlines' and jackpot! There she was. A few photos deep, and there was Emy. Chloe didn't share Emy's guarded privacy. He wasn't surprised but relieved.

He pulled out his phone and found Chloe on Instagram. He followed her and then sent off a direct message, hoping she would see it sooner than later.

JACKSON Hi Chloe, Jackson, or 1A, as you liked to call me. I hope you're doing well. Remember the napkin you gave me with Emy's number on it? Well, someone spilled espresso all over it at the cafe before I could finish typing Emy's number into my phone. The napkin was ruined, and I can't make out the number anymore. I tried to get to her at the airport before she left but couldn't. Can you please give her my number? Tell her I am so sorry, and I miss her terribly. Thanks, Jackson. 917-555-2226

Jackson was shocked he had hit send. This was the first time he'd been so open and transparent with his feelings. Now he had to hope Chloe was active enough on Instagram to see his message. Her last post was from two weeks ago. He prayed he didn't have to wait that long to hear back.

"Colleen, you're a lifesaver."

He got up and collected his bag. He bent over and gave Colleen a peck on the cheek.

"Not bad for someone more than twice your age. You must be in love. I can't believe in this age of social media, you didn't think to look her up."

She could see Jackson wasn't himself. Knowing him as long as she had, she knew he was more than a little bothered.

He gave her a huge hug before he left for the day. He was exhausted and needed to get some rest before he finished what he came to do. As of now, it looked like he'd be in Paris a few more days.

∞

JACKSON WAS MORE TIRED THAN HE THOUGHT. He slept for several hours. When he woke, he knew by now that Emy must have already landed in New York. He checked his Instagram account. Nothing. His message hadn't even been read yet. He didn't know how he would focus the next few days and felt like a fool "waiting" by the phone.

There was one other person he knew he could count on to find Emy. He would just have to take a punch in the gut to make it happen.

∞

"YOU'RE KIDDING ME, RIGHT?" Jessica was fourth in line among the Riley siblings. She was driven and smart and thirteen months older than Jackson. She also had no problem sharing her thoughts out loud. If she wasn't the gallery's interim curator, she would be in Paris as they spoke.

"This is so unlike you, Jack. I'm trying to figure out if this is a joke. Just so I fully understand, you met a flight attendant on the flight over to Paris, and you spent Christmas Day with her. Then, even though you left out this detail, I'm assuming you spent the night with her too. And though you had the time of your life, you never got her phone number at any point?"

"The fact that I'm calling you from Paris asking you for help should pretty much tell you I'm not joking, Jess."

Jackson was seated on the edge of his bed. The same bed he shared with Emy the night before. He got up and walked over to the open window, then stepped out onto the edge.

As he watched people descend into the Louvre, he said, "I told you, her phone died, but I had a napkin in hand with her phone number. Seemed pretty safe to me that I'd be able to get hold of her."

"You really can't make this up. You do realize phones have ways to add contact info for a reason, right?"

He knew he was going to take a beating from his sister. She was a realist and was all business. But she was also smart, and he knew she'd be helpful. He'd just have to take her jabs in the meantime. Feeling as though she'd given him enough grief, "What's her name?"

"Emerson Nichols."

Jessica started typing on the other end of the phone. Even though she had given Jackson a hard time, she was closest to him. She knew it took all of him to contact her, so she'd do whatever she could to help him.

"So, we have an Emerson Nichols, thirty-three, lives in the West Village, works for Infinite Airlines."

He could hear Jessica typing on the other end.

"How is she not on social? I mean, good for her. But it makes finding her a whole lot harder."

✈

29

Emy

EMY AND CHLOE SPENT SEVERAL DAYS TRYING ON DRESSES AT THE MOST PRESTIGIOUS BRIDAL SALONS IN THE CITY. Chloe had a specific dress in mind and had looked forward to the final fitting for months. She tried on a ton of dresses she knew she wasn't going to get, just as Emy had told her to do.

Emy was relaxed. She enjoyed a glass of Veuve while Chloe paced the room as they waited for the final dress to be brought out. Chloe had it special-ordered and hadn't yet seen it in person.

"Here it is!" the stylist said as she brought the bag over to Chloe. "It's going to look amazing on you."

With the dress draped over her arms, the stylist presented Chloe with the dress she had been pining for. Chloe found this dress months ago, but there was no guarantee it would arrive in time.

Chloe clapped her hands like a kid in a candy shop. The dress was exactly what she had hoped for. She was so happy she found Patrick and was finally getting her fairytale wedding, dress included. The stylist was right. She looked stunning in it.

Emy set down her champagne glass and stood up. She walked over to Chloe and stood next to her in the mirror.

"You look perfect." Both girls had tears in their eyes. "Seriously, Patrick is one lucky man. If he doesn't marry you, I will." And they both started laughing.

"This is it. You're right, it's perfect. And Patrick *is* lucky." Chloe winked at Emy. "Now, let's get this off of me because you're up next."

The day couldn't have gone better. Both girls found perfect dresses—Emy on the first try. Even with racks and racks of dresses to choose from, Emy went for a classic, simple style that complimented Chloe and her dress. It was going to be Chloe's big day. Emy didn't have an ego and wanted to make sure all eyes would be on Chloe as she walked down the aisle.

Both women left feeling radiant. Emy loved that they got to share this special moment together. It captured the essence of their friendship and the excitement of the upcoming day. Emy was relieved that the dress Chloe dreamed of worked out. Otherwise, today could have gone very differently.

The girls stepped outside the studio and walked back to the Village. It was a gorgeous day, so they decided to grab coffee for their walk back. They popped into the Starbucks Reserve before walking home.

"Oh! By the way, I need you for something else."

Chloe had just put way too much sugar in her coffee as she turned to Emy.

"I need a date."

Taking a sip of the hot coffee to taste it, she set it down to add even more sugar.

"I'm not dating anytime soon, Chloe." Emy looked over her shoulder at her. "Not even you."

Emy held her coffee close to warm herself up. She started back out the door, leaving Chloe behind.

Chloe pushed open the door and caught up to her.

"I just need you to be my date to an event Patrick is speaking at. I don't want to go alone. You know how these things are, super boring."

Chloe knew she would eventually give in. But with her current mood, it might take a bit more begging this time.

There was still no word from Jackson. As much as Chloe wanted to talk about it, she knew it was too fresh. It had been three days since they'd arrived back home. Getting Emy out had been harder than she had thought.

"Fine. What are we doing now? It had better be fun. And food. You have to feed me."

Emy was only half joking. She could use a night out, even if it was going as a plus one to a work event that wasn't even her own.

"I'll feed you, regardless. It's cocktail attire. But I promise we won't have to stay long. We already have a car. I'll pick you up tomorrow night at 7:00."

Chloe was practically skipping and spilling her coffee at the same time.

Sometimes Emy wondered how the two of them became such good friends. Chloe was nothing like her. Emy always thought things through and rarely made a quick decision. Chloe on the other hand was always in a hurry and didn't think twice before she jumped in with both feet.

She knew Chloe was trying to distract her, as she had gone to several events with Patrick before and held her own just fine. As a social butterfly, she could handle herself just about anywhere. Emy had watched Chloe in action, wishing she had more of Chloe's charm.

Maybe a night out was just what Emy needed. If anything, it would be fun to wear something other than her flight uniform.

30

Jackson

"IT LOOKS LIKE WE CAN FIND OUT MORE ABOUT EMY FROM HER FRIEND, CHLOE," JACKSON SUGGESTED. "Her Instagram profile isn't locked down."

Jessica was once again typing fast on the other end of the line.

"Hey J, I have to run. I have a meeting in a few minutes. When I have time today, I'll poke around and find out what I can."

Jessica and Jackson were the closest of the siblings, and she knew Jackson was a great catch. Whoever he ended up with would be one lucky woman. Before she hung up, she adjusted her tone.

"It's going to be okay. It might take a bit of time, but we'll find your girl."

Jackson thought he'd feel better after talking to Jess. But instead, he felt worse. The thought of Emy out there somewhere, thinking he didn't care enough to call or text drove him nuts. He wished he could let it go, but he kept checking his DMs, hoping for a reply from Chloe.

Nothing. He could only imagine how Emy felt before the flight, and it probably got worse when she landed in New York with nothing from him.

Jackson had an event later that evening. He was still feeling restless, so he decided to go for a run. His impromptu run took an unexpected turn, as he found himself standing below the Eiffel Tower. The rhythmic pounding of his footsteps led him to where it all began.

As he caught his breath, the Eiffel Tower stood tall, a testament to the timeless allure of the City of Light. For the second time, he found himself in disbelief that he hadn't visited this place more often.

As the sun started to set, it cast a golden hue over the architectural masterpiece. Jackson couldn't help but marvel at the intricate details that adorned its structure. The surroundings echoed with the sounds of the bustling city, blending harmoniously with the quiet reverence of the early evening hour.

Once again, memories of Emy rushed back. If it wasn't for her, he would never have appreciated this monument as much as he did now.

Not giving it a second thought, he pulled out his phone and clicked over to Instagram. Still no word from Chloe. She hadn't posted any updates since the last time he checked, but he decided to send off one more message in hopes it would reach her.

> **JACKSON** Hey Chloe, Jackson again. Just hoping you get this message. I feel horrible for not getting in touch with Emy and am really hoping you can help me out. I've been thinking of her since she left. Not sure if you got my last message or not, but I would love your help getting in touch with her.

Send. Once again, he prayed that Chloe would get his messages, sooner than later.

He needed to get back to the hotel. As he continued his run, the echo of his footsteps couldn't drown out the sound of Emy's voice in his head. When she asked him if he would have called her, he should have told her yes. Instead, he left her with doubt. Now he seemed like a selfish prick.

∞

AFTER A QUICK SHOWER, HE WAS READY FOR THE BLACK-TIE EVENT AT THE PARIS GALLERY. Before they packaged and shipped Lucy's pieces, they were having one last showing at the gallery. Local artists and exhibit designers would be on site. Normally Jackson would enjoy such an event. Truthfully, he just didn't want to be there, but he'd do it for Colleen.

He arrived later than he anticipated. The room was already full of various artists, curators, and spectators. He recognized a few friendly faces. His parents would be proud to know he was doing the job that normally fell on one of his older sisters.

Jackson loved his job, but today, he didn't want to be here. Although a lot older, the Paris gallery had a similar feel to their gallery back home. Being in this space always made Jackson feel at ease. He was grateful to be in a familiar place now. As he strolled around the room making as much small talk as he could, he heard his name being called.

"Jackson! So good to see you. Have you met Lucy?" Marcie Simon guided Jackson over to Lucy.

Marcie had worked with Colleen for years. Jackson considered her family as well. He was happy to see her, but could tell she also had intentions of connecting him with Lucy. She was going to be disappointed.

"Actually, we've already met. Lucy, nice to see you again."

Jackson was polite but kept his distance, knowing Colleen had intended to set the two of them up. That was before she had heard about Jackson's latest love interest. But the last thing he wanted to do was give off any vibe other than a professional working relationship.

"Jackson, nice to see you too."

Lucy walked closer to Jackson and hooked her arm through his.

"Walk with me."

They both left Marcie and found a more private spot of the room. Before he could get a word out, Lucy paused and turned to face him.

"Jackson, I'm afraid that Colleen and Marcie are worried that the two of us are unable to find partners on our own. Not to offend you, but I wanted to let you know that I'm seeing someone. She's here tonight, and I didn't want it to be awkward between us."

Jackson chuckled.

"You have no idea how relieved I am to hear that. You're incredible, and I think Colleen and Marcie have our best interests at heart, but I'm sort of seeing someone as well."

Both breathed sighs of relief.

"Can I get us both a drink now?"

Jackson was finally able to relax around Lucy. He enjoyed the evening and meeting her partner. For a brief hour or so, he almost forgot how panicked he was.

But being around Lucy and seeing how happy she was made him more determined than ever to find Emy.

31

Emy

IT WAS ALMOST 7:00 P.M. Emy was still trying to figure out what shoes to wear. She decided to go with the red sole shoes. They were higher than the others and added a few more inches to her 5-foot 5-inch frame. Just as she was struggling to get the second shoe on, her phone chirped.

That alert could only be Chloe, which meant she and Patrick were downstairs waiting for her. With one last look in the mirror, she pulled out her Channel lip gloss and applied a bright red coat to her lips.

"Go big or go home, I say! Right, Marie?"

With nothing to lose, she grabbed her clutch and headed out the door to the waiting car.

"Where's Patrick?" Emy slid into the car and noticed Patrick wasn't there. "Did he ditch you again?"

Emy joked with a giggle. She knew Chloe was always late, and it was always better to meet her wherever you were going instead of waiting for her. How Chloe made her call times as a flight attendant, no one could figure out.

"Of course he left me to get there early. Why do you think I wanted a plus one? The event started an hour ago. He knew I'd be late."

Both girls laughed because they knew it was true. Chloe was never on time, so she needed a date to walk in late with.

Poor Patrick was still getting used to the idea that his fiancée wasn't good at time management. He would have to show up to most events alone. Emy knew this by now, and it didn't faze her. Chloe checked herself in the mirror one more time before they pulled away.

Looking out the window, Emy wondered out loud, "Where are we going, anyway? You know my life is pathetic since I didn't even ask before I agreed to go with you."

"We're going to Tribeca. I think it's a gallery or something. Just around the corner from where JFK Jr. lived, according to Patrick."

"I was just happy for a reason to dress up for once. Plus, the promise of food will get me pretty much anywhere."

Emy realized she hadn't had anything to eat, so she was counting on something more than hors d'oeuvres. She enjoyed these events with Chloe and Patrick and wished she had her own partner to attend with. She loved an evening where she could dress up and feel like an adult.

∞

CHLOE POINTED OUT THE WINDOW, SIGNALING THEY HAD ARRIVED. As they got out of the car, both girls found the gallery mesmerizing.

The beautiful gallery was nestled in Manhattan's sought-after Tribeca area. The girls stepped through a sleek glass entrance. As they did, a path unfolded leading them through a sanctuary of artistic works. The polished concrete floors guided them in the direction of the party. Contemporary chandeliers hung from high ceilings, casting a warm ambiance, boosting each patron's appearance.

This was by far the fanciest event they had been to. Emy started to wonder if she had dressed appropriately.

"Jeez, you clean up nice," Emy pointed out, getting a better look at Chloe.

"Not bad yourself."

Chloe knew once she was officially married to Patrick, she needed to do better with Emy. Emy was her best friend and always stepped in when she was needed. Tonight was no exception.

"What kind of event is this?"

Emy looked around the room in disbelief. The space was remarkable and much nicer than any event she had been to before.

As they strolled through the gallery, they noticed the exposed-brick walls, which served as a canvas for the curated artwork on display. The open layout allowed for a seamless flow between exhibits. Tonight, they were allowed to wander the gallery before they were seated for dinner.

Scattered throughout the gallery were different seating areas, each adorned with plush velvet chairs and minimalist tables, providing intimate spaces for the cocktail hour. The vibe and energy were definitely Tribeca, but the overall feel of the gallery was warm and inviting.

"Chloe, I need a cocktail before I leave you."

Emy and Chloe discovered the bar at the same time as they scanned the room. Out of the corner of her eye, Emy noted the handsome man approaching them with two cocktail glasses in hand.

"Patrick. You are a mind reader."

Emy leaned in and gave Patrick an air kiss and side hug. She was always happy to see him. From the moment she first met him, she knew he was a keeper. Chloe and Patrick were perfect for each other.

"How are my two favorite ladies? On time as usual I see." He handed them their cocktails of choice.

"You'll be devastated to hear that you missed my presentation. You'll just have to spend the rest of the evening looking pretty, drinking these fancy cocktails, and enjoying dinner. Now, if you'll excuse me, I must mingle."

He leaned in and kissed Chloe before moving on.

"Jesus, Chloe. Do you know how lucky you are? I mean, he's lucky too, but man. That guy."

Emy raised her glass as Patrick floated away into the crowd. "You have no idea, Emy. I thank my lucky stars every single day." Chloe was looking in the direction Patrick had disappeared. "And it will happen for you too. You know that, right?"

Chloe clinked her glass to Emy's, and the girls sipped their cocktails.

Emy wasn't so sure anymore.

32

Jackson

IT WAS 1:00 A.M. IN PARIS. Jackson had picked up his phone several times over the last few hours. Once he and Lucy confessed to other love interests and agreed being set up was a very bad idea, the evening had passed smoothly.

Jackson still cut the evening short, just in case he got word from Jessica or heard back from Chloe. Neither had happened, but he was glad he had met up with Lucy at the gallery. He looked forward to showcasing her work in New York. She was even bringing her partner with her, so he looked forward to hosting both of them later next month.

He checked his phone again. It was 7:00 p.m. in New York. He wondered what Emy was doing. It had been three days since he had seen her, but it felt even longer. He thought he would have heard from Jess by now. Grabbing his phone again, he fired off a quick text.

"Any updates? I thought you worked faster than this?"

He had no idea what had come over him. He hadn't connected with anyone seriously in a long time. Until Emy. The second he laid eyes on her, he knew he wanted to be around her. Spending Christmas Day with her was incredible. He had told her it was one of his best first dates, but it was really *the* best.

Jackson heard his phone ping and grabbed it. The first text reply contained one word.

JESSICA Jerk.

Well, that could only be from one person. He knew Jess could be baited easily. Not a tactic he liked to use, but he needed information.

JESSICA I'm working. In case you forgot, our gallery is
open for business, and tonight we have a full house
of pediatricians. You'll have to wait. You're being a
big baby right now. You could probably learn something from these people.

Leave it to her to get the last word in.

She was right; he needed to leave her alone so she could get work done. It was still the holiday season, and he knew she was working overtime, picking up additional work so their sisters could spend time with their kids. Jessica was tough, but she respected her family. That meant she'd do anything for them, even if it meant working late nights at special events.

Jackson plugged in his phone. He needed to get some sleep. Tomorrow would be a long day overseeing the packaging of Lucy's art. If all went well, he might be home on New Year's Eve.

33

Emy

EMY AND CHLOE SAUNTERED AROUND THE ROOM. On their second cocktail, they made small talk with other attendees. Dinner would be served soon. As they turned toward their table, they caught Patrick motioning for them. He was speaking with someone they didn't know.

"Chloe, Emy, I want you to meet Jessica. She's one of the gallery owners. Jessica, this is my fiancé, Chloe, and her friend Emy."

Patrick had an appreciation for galleries and architecture. It was no surprise he found the person in charge of this amazing space. But the music had started, and the foursome could barely hear his introductions.

"Oh no, I'm not the owner. It's a family business for sure; I'm just the lucky one who has no kids, so I work the late shifts. No offense."

Jessica was kidding of course, but they all laughed.

"I'm actually the interim curator here while my sister is away. My other family members make the magic happen. I'm only slightly joking about my place in the hierarchy. My parents opened the gallery many years ago, and we've all been part of it our whole lives."

There was something about this woman that was so familiar. But as hard as she tried, Emy couldn't figure out where they might have met before.

"It's beautiful. A truly remarkable space," Emy noted confidently, as she couldn't take her eyes off Jessica.

Chloe was overjoyed at Emy's reaction. "We're glad you like it!"

Beaming, she grabbed Emy's hand. "We've secured it for our wedding. I wanted to surprise you. You're the first to know!"

"Are you serious? I love it! This is perfect. Oh, you guys. It's going to be such a beautiful day. I'm so happy I get to be part of it."

Chloe gave Emy a bear hug and pulled Patrick into the huddle.

"We are so glad it worked out." Jessica turned to the group. "If you're free one day soon, you should come back and see it when it's cleared out. I think you'd be impressed with how big the space really is."

"Are you free tomorrow?" Chloe asked.

Jessica laughed at Chloe's eagerness. "Let me double check my schedule, but I think tomorrow should work."

∞

AFTER DINNER, EMY CALLED AN UBER TO GET HOME. It was getting late, and she needed to make sure she was ready for her next trip. The idea of working New Year's Eve suddenly felt daunting.

At the time she posted her shift trade, she thought she was doing someone a favor. She couldn't have anticipated her current situation. She would much rather be at home hiding this year, rather than working another trip to Paris.

Just as the car pulled up to her apartment, she got a text from Chloe.

> **CHLOE** Emy! Want to see the gallery with me tomorrow morning before you head out? Jessica confirmed she could meet us here. I'd love for you to come back and see it with me in the daylight.

> **EMY** I'd love to, but I'm planning to get to the airport earlier than usual because of the holiday.

Emy didn't want to get caught up in the craziness of Times Square and would be taking a different route to JFK. The commute might take a little longer than usual.

CHLOE Understood. I'll send you photos tomorrow!

34

Jackson

JACKSON'S ALARM WAS GOING OFF. He hadn't slept in days and finally slept through the night. He had never been so glad to be finishing up a project. The only thing that had made the end of this week bearable was the people he worked with.

He got out of bed and took a quick shower, thinking this was possibly his last shower for this trip. He made sure his bag was packed and ready to go, just in case he finished earlier than anticipated.

Despite the length, nothing sounded better to him than a seven-hour flight back to New York.

35

Emy

EMY KNEW THE RIDE TO JFK WOULD BE LONG ON NEW YEAR'S EVE. Every year seemed to get crazier and crazier. Her flight left at 6:00 p.m., but she needed to be at the airport by 3:00 p.m. It was almost 11:00 a.m., and she planned on leaving around noon.

As Chloe's maid-of-honor, she felt guilty for not meeting her at the gallery today. Chloe said she would meet Jessica at the gallery at 11:00 a.m.

Technically, I could still go for a few minutes and still have time to get to the airport in time.

Emy sent Chloe a quick text…

EMY Hey, you at the gallery yet? I have a few extra
minutes, so I can join you there! On my way, but
warning, I'm in uniform since I'll need to go straight
to the airport.

CHLOE Yay! See you soon, friend. And thank you. I
know it's a crazy day for you.

Chloe had been at the gallery for just a few minutes. She let Jessica know that Emy would be joining them after all.

Emy grabbed a taxi since she had both her rollerboard and carry-on bag. It took longer than usual. Drivers were busy getting people to Times Square. Tribeca was only a mile away, but she knew it would take longer than usual to get there today.

∞

WHEN HER CAB ARRIVED AT THE GALLERY, THE STREETS WERE RELATIVELY QUIET. Emy was surprised the gallery was even open. It was just past 11:00 a.m., so she had almost an hour before she had to leave.

The outside of the gallery was just as beautiful in daylight as it had been the night before. The building was remarkable. She hoped it worked out for their wedding.

She opened the door and entered. She dropped her bags just inside the doorway. She didn't see anyone right away, but she heard voices coming from the back.

Emy took her time looking around the gallery as she walked toward the voices. The rooms were shaped by movable walls that accommodated different exhibits. She had always loved art. She spent a lot of time visiting museums and galleries around the world. But this space had something special about it that drew her in. The gallery looked very different with the morning light pouring through high windows.

Emy finally found Chloe and Jessica sitting at a table in the back. It was the only table remaining from the night before.

The two were drinking champagne. Emy guessed they were celebrating the signing of the wedding venue contract. Jessica was right; the space was very large. It would be perfect for the wedding.

"Well? Are we all set?" Emy approached their table and leaned in to give Chloe a side hug.

"We are! What do you think?" Chloe took a sip of her champagne. Knowing Emy couldn't drink any before her flight, Chloe had sparkling cider waiting for her.

"Jessica..." Chloe asserted, "You remember my friend Emerson from last night, right?"

Jessica stared at Emy from the moment she came into view.

Hold on! Emy is a flight attendant! Her name tag says Emerson!

The room was spinning. There was no way this was *the* Emerson her brother had cried about for several days. But then she remembered Emerson's friend was named Chloe. *The same*

Chloe her brother messaged. She looked very different from the Instagram photos.

Suddenly, everything became crystal clear. All her internet sleuthing no longer mattered.

After staring at both of them intently, Jessica started laughing uncontrollably. She grabbed her glass of champagne, finished it, and immediately filled it back up.

Emy and Chloe eyed Jessica with concern, trying to figure out what was so amusing and what had their host chugging very expensive champagne like it was water.

"Ladies, I'm going to need you to sit down. I have something to tell you, and you're not going to believe me. For the first time in my life, I'm dumbfounded."

Jessica grabbed the champagne and filled Chloe's glass to the rim. She wasn't sure how to get through this one.

Jessica took a deep breath and looked directly at Emy.

"My name is Jessica Riley. My brother is Jackson Riley. The same Jackson Riley who is currently in Paris licking his wounds because he managed to ruin a napkin with your phone number on it."

Emy's mouth fell open. She felt dizzy and sat down at the table, speechless. She knew Jessica looked familiar. But now she realized… it wasn't because they had met before. The family resemblance was uncanny. Now that she heard it directly, there was no denying this was absolutely Jackson's sister.

Jessica turned to Chloe.

"The same Jackson who sent you a DM on Instagram four days ago. He's been checking his phone countless times a day ever since."

She took another sip of champagne, then set her glass down and pulled out her own chair to sit down. The room was silent. As she took another drink, she patiently waited for their reactions.

Emy couldn't move. Chloe jumped up and grabbed her phone. "I haven't been on Instagram in weeks. I would never have seen a message there." As she tapped over to her DMs, there it was. "Holy crap, Emy. He messaged me before we took off from Paris."

Chloe handed her phone over to Emy so she could read it.

JACKSON Hi Chloe, Jackson, or 1A, as you liked to call me. I hope you're doing well. Remember the napkin you gave me with Emy's number on it? Well, someone spilled espresso all over it at the cafe, and before I could finish typing Emy's number into my phone. The napkin was ruined, and I can't make out the number anymore. I tried to get to her at the airport before she left but couldn't. Can you please give her my number? Tell her I am so sorry, and I miss her terribly. Thanks, Jackson. 917-555-2226

Emy read the second message that followed the next day.

JACKSON Hey Chloe, Jackson again. Just hoping you
get this message. I feel horrible for not getting in
touch with Emy and am really hoping you can help
me out. I've been thinking of her since she left. Not
sure if you got my last message or not but would
love your help getting in touch with her.

He had tried to reach her for days. No one could talk. How was this possible? Chloe picked up her glass and drank it down too. Jessica finally broke the silence.

"This is unbelievable. First off, I just have one question. How do you sleep with someone and not get their number?"

They all started laughing. But Emy's laughter turned into a stream of happy tears. She had spent the last week thinking Jackson didn't want to see her again. But according to Jessica, this was far from the truth.

"He called me in the middle of the night asking for help finding you, Emy. When he realized he didn't have a way to reach you, he rushed to the airport prepared to buy a ticket for any flight, just to get to you. But he left his passport at the hotel, so they wouldn't sell him a ticket."

Jessica relayed the bits and pieces of what he had gone through all week to try to find Emy.

"It didn't help that you have almost zero social media presence. It wasn't until I saw you in uniform and heard your name that the connection hit me. Then I remembered finding Chloe online."

Looking over at Chloe, Jessica continued, "You, on the other hand, are an open book. But you look nothing like most of your pictures. Maybe that's why I didn't recognize you until now."

Jessica settled back down in her chair.

"He texted me last night asking for an update. I just hadn't had a chance yet to find you, Chloe. We figured once we found you, we'd eventually be able to find Emerson more easily."

"Emerson, are you alright?" Chloe moved to sit closer to her.

Emy looked like she was sick. She looked at her watch and jumped up.

"Oh my god, you guys, I'm going to be late. Figure things out and text me."

Emy gave quick hugs to both women and headed for the door. She'd have to be lucky to make it to JFK on time.

"Emy! Wait, I have an idea. Where's your crew bag?"

She grabbed her bag and handed it to Chloe, who rummaged through it as if her life depended on it.

"*Yes*! Perfect."

Chloe found what she hoped for. She handed the bag back to Emy, saw her off, and got to work.

∞

EMY WAS IN A CAB HEADING TO JFK, HOPING JUST TO GET THERE ON TIME. She was in shock and didn't even know how to process what had happened. It was unbelievable.

The last thing she wanted to do right now was go work on a flight.

∞

BACK AT THE TRIBECCA GALLERY, CHLOE LOOKED AT JESSICA.

"I'll need your brother's phone number."

Both girls formed sinister grins. Nothing could have prepared them for this day and the turn of events that had just taken place.

36

Jackson

Jackson was up early and at the gallery with Colleen, Marcie, and Lucy. They were in full packing mode. Each piece had to be packaged and cataloged with care and precision. Jackson was in his element, working fast, trying to get everything done.

Regardless of what was happening in his personal life, he planned to have everything wrapped up in time for everyone to spend New Year's Eve with their families. As of now, everything was going as planned.

"Jackson, what are your plans tonight?" Lucy asked.

He had been so focused on getting things ready to go at the gallery, he hadn't had time to think about New Year's Eve plans. That wasn't entirely true, though. He had briefly thought he would have found a way to spend it with Emy if he had the chance. But that wasn't going to happen now.

"No plans officially. I usually spend it with my sister's kids. If we're done here, I'm hoping to catch a flight home tomorrow, so I'll probably stay in."

If he could get home tomorrow, that was his primary plan. However, he knew he might have to settle for the hotel bar, drinking a glass of complimentary champagne.

"Come out with us for a little bit. We'll have you back home at a reasonable time. It would be a shame to be alone tonight."

Lucy packed up the last of the boxes and moved them beside the shipping door.

"Seriously, just for a little bit. It's Paris, for heaven's sake. We'll watch the fireworks over the Tower. You won't be disappointed, I promise."

"I'm not sure I'll last until the fireworks, but I'll join you for a little bit."

Jackson was just relieved they had finished in reasonable time. It had been a long week, and he just wanted to be back home.

∞

HE MET UP WITH LUCY AND HER PARTNER AT A SPOT CLOSE TO HIS HOTEL. They enjoyed champagne and toasted to the New Year and the partnership with the gallery. They talked about what to do when Lucy came to New York.

As it neared midnight, he decided it was best to leave and walked back to the hotel alone. Even though he had only been here a few days, his stay in Paris felt much longer. The stress of the week had him feeling spent.

Walking back to the hotel, Jackson pulled out his phone and saw a missed call from Jessica. It was 6:00 p.m. in New York. He could still give her a call but decided she didn't need to hear from him tonight. She was probably already out with friends, so he sent her a quick text instead.

JACKSON Hey sis, Happy New Year. Hoping to come home tomorrow. See you soon.

He saw the three little bouncing dots from Jessica. She responded right away.

JESSICA Sorry, bro. You'll need to stay at least one more day. Be at the Paris gallery at 10:00 a.m. tomorrow. Problem with the shipment. See you soon.

Dammit. She wasn't texting with an update. Instead, she dropped a bomb on him that he had to stay one more day. Every day he wasn't home was one more day he was farther from finding Emy. Just when he thought he couldn't be more depressed.

He entered the hotel lobby, grabbed a glass of complimentary champagne, and headed to his room. The concierge held the elevator for him.

"Happy New Year, friend" Jackson said as he stepped into the waiting elevator.

"To you too, sir. I hope this year brings everything you wish for."

The elevator door closed; Jackson leaned back against the wall.

"Not sure that's going to happen," he said out loud to himself before he tossed back his glass of champagne.

When he got to his hotel room, he noted the bags he had already packed, so he'd be ready to leave first thing in the morning. That wasn't going to happen after all.

What a way to celebrate the New Year!

37

Emy

EMY'S HEAD WAS STILL SPINNING, AND SHE HADN'T HAD ANY
CHAMPAGNE. She had to get a cab to the airport since she was
running late now. Once on her way to JFK, she pulled out her
phone and saw a group chat with Chloe and Jessica. The three
of them had come up with a plan for when Emy arrived in Paris.
Now she just had to wait and see if it would work.

Attached in the text message was a shared contact for
"Jackson Riley." Emy added his info to her contacts. As part of
the plan, Emy made Chloe and Jessica promise they would not
contact Jackson until she did. She wanted to ensure he heard
from her first.

Emy felt like the weight of the world was lifted. She had
been sad. But she didn't know how much she cared about
Jackson until she knew they would see each other again for sure.

She was amazed at the lengths he had gone to try to find her. It never crossed her mind that something prevented him from reaching her. She pulled out her phone again and looked at the selfie they took together.

Emy sat back in the cab and grinned in anticipation. *I'm on my way, Jackson!*

She arrived at the airport in time for her crew briefing. She was thrilled to see Allen and Jeff again. Hugging Allen tight, she thanked him for being such a good friend to her on the last flight.

"You know you saved me on our flight home from Paris. I can't thank you enough."

"Anything for you, my friend."

Allen noted that she seemed in much better spirits than after their last trip together.

She had an unbelievable story to tell once they were on the plane. Emy was trying to be professional; she couldn't stand still. She couldn't wait to get on the plane and fill her friends in on what had happened just hours before. Both men knew something was happening. The last time they saw her, she was really unhappy.

It was almost New Year's in Paris. Emy wouldn't get to spend New Year's Eve with Jackson, but she'd definitely be starting the New Year with him.

Emy, Allen, and Jeff were working up front again. The three of them stowed their bags as she filled in Allen and Jeff.

"In all my years of flying, I've never heard anything so unbelievable," Allen remarked.

The catering truck had just pulled away, and they were trying to get the first-class galley ready. Emy poured champagne while Allen pulled out glasses for juice and water. As she told them the entire story, Allen finally understood the shift in her demeanor. Emy was happy.

Jeff was shocked too. "So, what are we doing now?"

They were both completely invested now, and they wanted to know what she was doing once they landed in Paris.

Emy was still trying to figure out the details herself. They were supposed to land at 7:45 a.m. local time. Jessica already communicated to Jackson that there was a problem at the gallery, and he needed to be there at 10:00 a.m. That kept him in Paris and gave Emy time to figure out a plan. The last thing she wanted was for him to get on a flight back to New York without her.

The flight seemed unbelievably long. Emy was too anxious and didn't think she'd be able to rest during her break. But when it was her turn for break, she was exhausted. The stress and worry of the past week finally caught up to her.

She thought she had only closed her eyes for a minute when her alarm started chirping.

"You were sleeping like a rock! I wish I could do that."

Ava Taylor was a new-hire flight attendant, working her first international flight. Emy remembered those early days and how stressful they were.

"Don't worry. One day you'll be so exhausted, you'll be snoring away your break."

Emy got up and freshened up for the last service before landing. She had butterflies in her stomach, thinking about seeing Jackson again soon. According to Jessica, Jackson would be just as excited to see Emy again as she was him.

Emy walked into the galley, and Jeff handed her a cup of coffee. "Boy, this feels familiar, doesn't it."

Allen had told Jeff about the flight home and how miserable Emy was.

"I'm hoping this has a better outcome than last week."

She felt guilty for dragging Allen down with her.

Allen popped into the galley and took the other coffee Jeff had placed on the counter for him.

"I'm really glad I have you two. Please don't ditch me."

Emy held her cup close to her face and gave a pouty look that neither of them could resist.

"We'd never ditch you. You keep us old guys on our toes." Allen winked at her, then picked up the tray of coffee to begin the beverage service.

Once the service was over, they'd be on the ground in less than an hour.

Emy couldn't wait. Before they took off, they had a plan in place. Now everything had to come together.

She was anxious and needed to keep moving. She headed back to economy to see if she could help pick up trash or clean up. This was why she loved flying with Chloe. The two always had something to talk about, which made the flight time pass quickly.

Emy walked through the cabin, picked up remaining service items, and headed to the back galley.

Pulling back the curtain, she saw Ava sitting quietly on the jumpseat while the more senior flight attendants were catching up. Emy pulled out the trash cart and put the trash away. She knew almost everyone on the flight and continued making small talk with them.

Out of the corner of her eye, she could see Ava listening in. Emy remembered what it was like being the new girl and shifted over to where Ava was seated.

"How ya doing, Ava?"

She pulled down the jumpseat next to Ava and got comfortable.

"I'm okay." She could tell Ava was far from okay. "It's just a little lonely when you're new."

Emy chuckled. She remembered all too well what it was like being new and alone on those first few trips. If she hadn't met Chloe in training, and if her mother hadn't prepared her, she wouldn't have survived.

"The first few months are hard. It's partly how they know who will stick around and who'll quit." Emy looked over at her. "You don't look like a quitter, Ava."

Ava looked down at the floor.

"Thanks. I hope I'm not. I was one of the only ones from my training class to come to New York. So, I really don't know anyone. The crash pad I'm staying at is horrible. Maybe once I find a new place, things will improve."

Emy got up from her seat.

"You know, Ava, you can call me anytime. I met my best friend, Chloe, flying for Infinite. You just need to find your person. Before long, you'll be having the time of your life and picking trips with your own friends."

Emy reached over and touched Ava's arm. "Hang in there; it'll get better. I promise."

She gave Ava a smile before she walked back up front, grateful for the distraction. She felt for Ava, but Emy had bigger things coming up that needed attention right now.

Smiling, she pulled back the first-class curtain and saw Jeff and Allen preparing the galley for landing.

"Are we there yet?" she asked them.

38

Jackson

JACKSON COULDN'T SLEEP NO MATTER HOW HARD HE TRIED. He had his bag packed, ready for the first flight home. He was doubtful that chance would be today since he had to be at the gallery at 10:00 a.m.

It was officially New Year's Day. Most everything around him would be closed.

He looked at the clock and noted it was just before 7:00 a.m. He had plenty of time to kick off the New Year with a run, just like everyone else setting new fitness goals. He had run every day this week, trying to take his mind off things. So far, it hadn't worked. But he'd try again today.

As he followed the same route as the day before, he thought that today felt warmer, and the sun was trying to come out. He chuckled.

Of course, the day I get ready to leave, the weather finally improves.

He was just a few yards from the hotel when he noticed an airline crew driving up to the hotel. Funny how he had never noticed crew member shuttles before. Now, he had to look away as he thought about Emy.

He needed this run now more than ever. Hopefully the crew members would be long gone from the lobby by the time he returned. The last thing he needed was another reminder of why he was so miserable.

39

Emy

AS HER CREW VAN ARRIVED AT THE HOTEL, EMY GRINNED CONFIDENTLY. Her plan was in place. But first, she wanted to shower and change.

Thanks to Jessica and Chloe, Jackson would be in for the surprise of his life. She just had to be in the right place at the exact time.

When she turned on her phone, she had a dozen messages in the text thread with Chloe and Jessica. Apparently, they were all going to be fast friends. She loved that Jessica was already rooting for and helping her.

Emy had no idea where Jackson was at the moment. She needed to check in, then get out of the lobby as fast as she could. They had waited this long; she didn't want anything to spoil the surprise.

Once she got her key, she hurried to her room. She had specifically asked to be on the fourth floor, hoping Jackson was still in the same room as before. She suddenly felt overwhelmed with emotion.

Nope, you're not doing that. You've been waiting a week to see him again. No going back now.

She sent the text to Jessica, putting everything in motion, then hopped in the shower.

About now, he should be getting a text from Colleen to meet him at the Café de la Tartine instead of the Gallery.

If everything went as planned, Emy had less than an hour before she reunited with Jackson.

40

Jackson

JACKSON ROUNDED THE FRONT CORNER OF THE HOTEL
AND FELT HIS PHONE VIBRATE IN HIS POCKET. It was a text
from Colleen.

> **COLLEEN** Bonjour, Jackson! Can you meet me at Café
> de la Tartine? I'll bring the new paperwork that
> needs to be attended to. Shouldn't take long. Merci!

This change sounded good to Jackson. It would save him
time since the café was closer to the hotel. Although he felt a
little uneasy about returning to the beginning and the end of
his story with Emy.

He hurried up to his room to get ready. He took a quick
shower, dressed, and headed out toward the café. He knew

Colleen would be prompt and would likely have a table waiting for them. Looking at his watch one more time, he wished he could fly home tonight.

Walking to the café, he loved the beautiful day it was turning out to be. It almost made him wish he was staying. But the sooner he returned home, the sooner he could try to find Emy.

As he entered the café, he looked around for Colleen. Ironically, she was seated with her back against the wall in the same seat he had sat with Emy and Chloe just last week. He walked over to the table and took the seat facing her.

"Oh, Jackson, thank you for meeting me this morning. I know you wanted to get home, but this just couldn't wait. I made a mistake on one of the shipping notices. You'll just need to verify the correction and sign off on the new notice."

Colleen handed over the documents. "It was actually Jessica who found the mistake. Leave it to her to always be one step ahead of us."

Jackson must be losing his mind. He couldn't see the error or any differences in the shipping notice. Colleen seemed a little off this morning, but he didn't want to make a big deal of it. Without hesitating, he signed the new bill.

"Thank you so much. We should be all set now. It was so good seeing you. Please give my love to your family."

Colleen got up even before the coffee had arrived.

Out of politeness, he pushed back his chair and started to rise.

"Don't get up; I'll see myself out."

Colleen leaned down and gave Jackson air kisses on both cheeks. He was completely thrown off but said his goodbyes.

"Goodbye my friend, I hope to see you again soon."

He gave Colleen's hand a squeeze thinking something wasn't right and making a mental note that he should talk to his parents about Colleen when he returned home.

Jackson thought he felt the barista brush his shoulder. He didn't bother looking up as she placed a napkin down on the table before him.

"I think you misplaced your napkin, sir."

Glancing down, he first noted the Infinite Airlines logo. Then his eyes found handwritten text that read, *Emerson Nichols, 917-555-1325.*

In disbelief, he shot around to find Emy beaming down at him. He almost fell out of his chair.

Emy stood beside Jackson, who jumped up from his seat and grabbed her like his life depended on it. She smelled just as he remembered. He wanted to say something, but he couldn't get the words out.

He couldn't breathe in the vastness of emotion he was now experiencing. Like Emy, he had been under enormous stress this week, worrying how he would ever find her again. Her surprise appearance melted away every worry as he inhaled the smell of her hair.

He pulled back and held Emy's face in his hands.

"God, I've missed you! This can't be real?"

Before she could say another word, he leaned in and brushed his lips to hers.

He grabbed Emy by the collar of her jacket and deepened the kiss. He had waited too long to be gentle and wanted her to know how much he had missed her.

"Do you still have your room at the hotel?" she whispered.

He didn't even answer her. Instead, he grabbed his jacket off the back of the chair and pulled her to the door. They exited in the direction of the hotel.

"How did you know where I'd be?"

Jackson was in shock. He wanted to know everything that had happened this past week. But first he needed her to know how sorry he was. He stopped, not letting go of Emy's hand. He turned to her.

"I can't even begin to tell you how sorry I am. You are all I have thought about since the moment—"

"I know. I know everything. I even know you tried to buy a ticket for a random flight just to say goodbye to me, which is nuts. In some crazy fateful way, I met your sister, Jessica. She filled me in on everything that's happened. All I've thought about since then is getting back to you."

"Jessica? You met Jessica in New York? Never mind, you can tell me later."

He would get the details later, but for now, he just wanted to get Emy back to the hotel room.

41

Emy

EMY COULDN'T BELIEVE THEY PULLED IT OFF. Chloe rewrote Emy's name and number on an Infinite Airlines napkin they found in her carry-on bag. And Emy kept it in her pocket the entire flight.

Jessica contacted Colleen, filled her in on the latest news, and asked her to figure out a way to keep Jackson on the ground just a bit longer. If she could keep him there until 10:00 a.m., there wouldn't be a flight home that day, making sure Emy would be able to catch him in Paris. Colleen was thrilled to be part of the plan and promised to do her best.

As they walked back to the hotel, Emy asked Jackson for his cell phone.

"We need to make sure we don't lose each other again."

Emy added her name and number into his phone, then marked her as one of his favorites with a heart emoji next to her name.

"Your sister had some choice words for you. I don't think I want to hear what she'd say if we got separated again."

He laughed and slid his phone back into his pocket. They were steps away from the hotel. She couldn't wait to get inside.

They walked into the hotel lobby together, then made a mad dash to the elevator. Once the elevator doors closed, he pushed Emy against the wall and kissed her.

She wanted him so badly; she welcomed the feel of his entire body pushing into her. He undid the belt holding her trench coat shut. He slid his hand inside her jacket, up under her sweater.

"Good God, Emy." Jackson paused long enough to catch his breath, "You're all I've been thinking about for a week!"

He reached up and smoothed out her hair as the elevator came to a stop. The doors opened. He didn't have to ask her if she wanted to come with him this time. They both knew where they were going.

∞

WHEN THEY GOT TO JACKSON'S ROOM, HE COULDN'T GET THE DOOR OPEN FAST ENOUGH. Once inside, Emy pulled him to her with an undeniable urgency and desire. She started to remove his clothes, one item at a time. They were back where it all began, but this time there was an undeniable need.

Jackson took in every inch of her. He let his eyes roam her body. She unbuttoned his shirt and peeled it away. Her hands roamed over his chest and up around his neck. She pulled him to her and kissed him, not wanting to let him go.

He took hold of Emy's hands and kissed them. He seemed to be doing his best not to rush things, but she wanted to get all clothes off as fast as possible.

He drove her crazy, and she just wanted him to touch her all over. Peeling her jacket off, he tossed it over the chair. Then he pulled her shirt over her head. He moaned, and she stood before him with her perky breasts peeking out behind her black bra.

Although she had only been with Jackson once before, she missed how her body reacted to him. He pulled closer to Emy; she wanted to taste him again.

She pulled away from him just long enough to rip his shirt over his head. She started kissing her way down his neck as she guided him over to the bed.

Emy was desperate for him. She pushed him back and unzipped his jeans. She could tell he watched her every move. She felt very lucky to be back with him.

Emy reached into his pants and pulled out his throbbing erection. Before he had a chance to speak, Emy's lips were already parted. She kneeled down before him, taking in the head of his penis. She held onto his shaft as she continued to tease the tip of his penis before taking all of him into her mouth. Jackson moaned as she teased him relentlessly.

She looked up at him as she swirled her tongue around the head of his penis. He grabbed her hair in fistfuls as he cried out her name. He let his head fall backward as Emy used her teeth.

Before he could finish, he grabbed Emy and pulled her up. He yanked down her bra so her nipples were exposed. He sucked and bit her nipples. Emy let out soft moans, holding on to him tightly.

He turned Emy over onto her stomach, then climbed onto the bed from behind her, sliding his body over the top of hers. His erect penis found the opening between her thighs.

"Don't move."

He flipped over temporarily, found a condom, and slipped it on. He rolled back to Emy where he left off and slid into her from behind.

She gasped as Jackson began moving in and out of her. He thrust slowly until he heard her breath quicken. She grabbed the pillow as she let out a small cry. She was so happy to be with him. They were in bed, together, again.

Both were on the verge of climax. Emy begged Jackson for more as he reached around and cupped her breast, pulling on her erect nipple with one hand and balancing for the both of them on the other. He had found the perfect rhythm. Just when she couldn't take it anymore, she cried out his name. He followed right behind her, finishing inside her.

Out of breath, he collapsed on top of her. He adjusted his weight to the side, avoiding Emy's petite frame. She didn't want to separate from him just yet.

Pushing her hair to the side, he gently kissed her shoulder. He stroked his hand up and down her back as he tried to steady his breath.

She turned over and wrapped her leg around his. She put her hand on his chest and felt his heart still beating heavily. For the first time in a long time, Emy felt loved.

42

Jackson

IT WAS HARD TO BELIEVE THEY HAD ONLY BEEN BACK IN THE HOTEL ROOM FOR A FEW HOURS. It was early in the afternoon when Jackson reached over and made sure Emy was still with him. He loved that she was sound asleep next to him. They had stayed in bed most of the day and had no need to go anywhere.

Trying not to wake her, he picked up his phone and texted Jess.

JACKSON Thank you.

He put his phone down, then rolled over to Emy as she started to stir.

"Hi." She reached up and brushed his hair from his forehead.

"Hi, yourself."

He felt his penis harden, just being next to her. He rolled over on top of her and started kissing her neck. Emy reached up and put her arms around his neck.

"Are you okay with this, or should we try to go outside to find dinner?"

"Why can't we do both, just not at the same time?" she proposed as she found his mouth with her tongue.

He reached up and wrapped his hand around Emy's neck, pulling her to him to deepen their kiss.

She slid her hands up his back and into his hair. "This is one of my favorite spots on you."

As she continued to roam his body, she drove him nuts. He wanted to spend more time exploring her body, but if he didn't do something quick, he wouldn't last as long as he'd like. He grabbed her hand and started pulling her up.

"What are we doing?" she asked sleepily.

"We're taking a shower."

He pulled Emy into the bathroom. Still holding her hand, he reached in and turned on the water. He held her close and began kissing her forehead, moving down to her lips, and then her neck. Then he pulled her into the steamy shower.

With his tousled brown hair, he stood with her under the gentle flow of hot water. His face relaxed as the warmth of the shower embraced them. He pulled Emy closer to him, and her eyes met his in a playful exchange.

As streams of water traced paths down their bodies, they shared soft kisses. As water flowed, they held onto each other as though they couldn't let go.

With ease, he picked up Emy. She wrapped her legs around his waist as he pushed her against the shower wall. He kept his lips on hers as her hands wandered up and down his back.

As the shower continued to heat up, his penis couldn't take much more.

"Emy, I want to be inside you again."

He kissed her neck and held onto her tight.

She pulled back from him so she could look him in his eyes.

"Jackson, I want you. All of you. I haven't been with anyone in the last two years. You're the only one. I'm on birth control."

"Are you sure? I haven't been with anyone in a long time either."

"Yes, I'm sure."

He positioned himself so he could lower her onto his cock.

She tilted her head and kissed him as the two became one. Emy clung to him while he continued to please them both.

Hearing her call out his name as she climaxed was such a turn-on. He threw his head back as he finished inside her.

Water droplets lingered on their skin. They emerged from the shower, cleansed by the water and renewed by the profound connection they had just shared. He grabbed two towels off the rack, and they dried off.

Jackson had never felt this close to someone before. He looked over at Emy as they started to get dressed.

"As much as I just want to stay here in the room with you all day, I think I should take you on a second date."

"Are you asking for one?" Emy questioned as she reached up and kissed him sweetly on the cheek.

✈

43

Emy

EMY AND JACKSON SPENT THE REST OF THE DAY EXPLORING THE CITY AND ENJOYING EACH OTHER'S COMPANY. She was finally able to explain to him how she had met his sister at their family gallery.

"The more I think about it, the more unbelievable it is. Never once did I think that could be the Tribeca gallery you had talked about."

They walked along the Seine, eating handheld crepes.

"And now, Chloe and Patrick are getting married there."

She continued to rave to Jackson how much she loved the space and that she couldn't wait for Chloe's wedding.

"As soon as I walked into the gallery, I fell in love with it. It was warm and inviting, I felt at home. And I wonder why?" When he looked over to her, she gave him a quick kiss on the cheek.

As they continued down the river, she asked about his relationship with Jessica.

"She loves you. I can tell that for sure. Although, for a second, I was a little scared of her," Emy admitted, laughing.

Jackson laughed too. She was pretty accurate for only meeting Jessica a couple of times now.

"We're close. She's very protective of me." He looked down at Emy as they walked.

"She's going to like you. A lot." He could already tell that Emy and Jess would become fast friends.

The day was coming to an end. They had spent the entire morning in bed and the afternoon walking the city together.

Walking hand in hand, they had just reached the hotel when they saw Allen and Jeff.

"Hey guys!" Emy had a huge smile on her face. "You might remember 1A from our Christmas flight. This is *Jackson*."

Her cheeks turned red from embarrassment. Allen and Jeff were her airline family, and she was excited for them to officially meet Jackson.

Jackson shook hands with the men, and they talked for a few minutes about what and where they were coming in from. Both men could see how relieved Emy was. She was smiling and had a glow about her.

They could also tell Jackson was thrilled. A far cry from the first time they had met him onboard the flight over to Paris. This was a changed man.

"Jackson, will we see you on the flight tomorrow?" Allen asked.

"Absolutely!" Jackson confirmed as he picked up Emy's hand and kissed it.

They said goodnight to Allen and Jeff, then found their way over to the elevator.

"Jackson, I want to stay the night with you, but I really need to sleep." she laughed. "Think we can do that? Just sleep?"

He put his arm around Emy's shoulder as they walked to his room.

"I'd like that."

✈

44

Jackson

JACKSON FINALLY HAD A FULL NIGHT OF REST FOR THE FIRST TIME SINCE BEFORE CHRISTMAS. "Should I walk back to your room with you?" He didn't want to separate from Emy, even if it would only be for an hour.

"No. Meet me downstairs." She assured him it would be fine.

"You're going to ride with us in the crew van. There's plenty of room, and I already got it approved. You've met Jeff and Allen, and I'm sure the rest of the crew is eager to meet you too."

Her eyes twinkled. She gave him a quick kiss and wink as she left his room to get ready for their flight home.

He was lucky to get one of the last seats on Emy's flight home. And he was eager to return to New York and start his life with her. No one ever had an effect on him like Emy. Even Jess had texted him back, advising him not to mess this up because she liked Emy more than she liked him. This was a first for Jess, as she was a hard one to impress.

It was officially the New Year, and things had taken a turn for the better over the last twenty-four hours. Emy was more than he could ever imagine in a partner. In between making love to one another, they spent the day discussing their plans.

Neither of them had ever dated seriously because they didn't see the point of wasting time, dating just to date. It had been a long road for both of them, and it was only fitting they had found each other now.

He took his bag off the bed and rolled it toward the door. This time, he was less eager to get home. He had enjoyed his time in Paris with Emy and couldn't wait to return here with her when neither of them was working.

Looking into the room one last time, he closed the door behind him and happily headed down to the lobby.

45

Emy

WATCHING JACKSON BOARD THE PLANE AND TAKE HIS SEAT PUT
EMY AT EASE. She couldn't help but smile, knowing that he was
once again seated in 1A.

She had switched positions with a junior flight attendant
who was happy to work in the back of the plane to let Emy be
in the front with Jackson. After hearing their story in the van,
who wouldn't have traded spots with her?

As she worked the cabin, she noticed Jackson fast asleep.
How different things were from when she had first met him. She
walked over to his seat and pulled the blanket up around him.

He was so handsome. His hair always ended up messy
when he slept, and she couldn't resist moving it out of his face.

As soon as she returned to the galley, Jeff asked, "Are we all happy with this outcome? Think of what it would have been like flying with her for the next year. Oof."

Emy rolled her eyes as she grabbed a cup from the galley cart.

"I'm not going to lie, Emy; that last flight home was painful." Allen stood in the doorway eating his lunch. "And I might have swapped off the next shift if you were still on it. There's no way I was flying one more mile with you, sweet girl—not like that."

He was only half joking, as his heart had legitimately ached for her. He was so relieved that things were right again. He couldn't remember a time over the last decade when he had seen her so at ease and carefree. His fatherly heart was happy for her.

"I wasn't that bad!" Emy cried. "Well, maybe I was. But you can see why, right? God, he's hot."

She moved back the galley curtain just enough to get a glimpse of Jackson, still sleeping.

"Not to mention smart, kind, thoughtful. *This* is what I've been waiting for, you guys. You've always told me not to settle, and I didn't. This was worth every bit of the drama it took to get here."

Emy closed the galley curtain and leaned against the counter. *Definitely worth the wait.*

✈

46

Jackson

JACKSON WAS IN THE PERFECT SPOT. He had the last seat in first class and would be able to talk with Emy when she wasn't busy. What he hadn't anticipated was falling asleep as soon as they took off. Apparently, the lack of sleep had finally caught up to him. When he finally did wake up, they were almost to New York.

He noticed the blanket had been pulled up around him. That must have been Emy's doing. He loved the comfort of her being close by while he slept.

He pulled his seat up from the reclined position and got up to visit the galley. He was now familiar with the voices coming from behind the curtain.

He pulled back the curtain and had a moment of déjà vu, looking across the galley at Emy. This time, he allowed a full smile to complement his messy hair.

Emy walked over to where Jackson stood.

"Looks like someone finally woke up while the rest of us were hard at work." She winked at him. "Are you hungry?"

Emy had saved a tray of food for him.

"Not really. I think I'm too excited to be heading home."

He looked around the galley and noticed they were alone. Somehow, Jeff snuck out to give the two of them privacy.

"Emy?" Jackson leaned on the galley doorway, staring at her. "If you're not doing anything tonight, I'd like to take you out on date number three."

She smiled big. "I can't wait!"

Epilogue

ONE YEAR LATER...

"We're going to be late if you don't hurry up." Emy held the door open for Jackson as he moved past her, holding bags of gifts.

She swatted his butt as he passed by, then gawked at him as he made his way past her. Letting the door close behind her, she bounded down the stairs to join him.

"If you hadn't bought so many gifts, we'd be there already."

He tried to navigate the stairs while carrying all the gifts they had bought for his nieces and nephews. They were headed to his oldest sister's house for Christmas.

It was starting to snow. Just enough to create a mess. But the kids would be happy to see a white Christmas.

"Did you get the last text? They need us to pick up several more things."

She looked at her phone and the text thread with all his sisters. Thanks to Jessica, she had instantly become part of the family. Emy, Jess, and Chloe had spent a lot of time together over the last year as well. They had become close friends.

"Yes, I saw the text," he confirmed. "This is how I know we're not late. They aren't even ready for us. We'll get five more texts before we get there."

Jackson had just finished putting the rest of the things in the car. He stood up straight and stared at Emy as she paused. She was trying to make sure they didn't forget anything.

As he looked over at her, he felt so lucky to be with Emy. She was perfect. The last year had been the best year of his life.

"Wait, I forgot something."

Jackson ran back up the stairs into the apartment.

She stood on their stoop, also thinking about the past year. Once home from Paris, the two of them had been inseparable. Their lives had merged as though they were always meant to be together.

Emy and Marie moved into Jackson's apartment a few months ago. Marie settled in quickly with all the new space available to her. Emy was still adjusting but loved waking up with Jackson every morning.

Jackson quickly adjusted to Emy's schedule. The two looked forward to reconnecting each week after she had been away for work.

This was the first Christmas she wasn't flying. It was also the first Christmas she would be spending with Jackson and his family. Just one year earlier, she had longed for such an event. And here she was, starting a new Christmas tradition with the Riley family.

Emy stopped taking additional trips and was flying just the airline's minimum hours. She started spending time at the gallery and learning about the art world from the Riley family. She traveled with Jackson on several trips and loved learning from him. Watching him at work was one of her favorite things to do.

Emy added a whole new feel to the gallery when she was there. People loved connecting with her and started to ask for her by name. She wasn't ready to give up her wings yet, but she loved hanging out with Jackson and his family.

Emy's parents returned in the spring to officially turn over their apartment to her. They decided they would slow down and move to the Carolinas, and they knew they wouldn't return to New York, except to visit. They still wanted to travel but wanted to have a place to call home.

Her parents adored Jackson and loved seeing Emy so happy. They all had plans to spend the New Year together before her parents headed out on their next adventure.

Before eventually moving in with Jackson, Emy finally accepted a new roommate. Ava Taylor moved in with her, and she took Ava under her wing.

Ava had had a rough start at Infinite Airlines but finally found her groove. Emy was happy to have someone she could trust taking care of the only home she'd ever known.

"Emy?" Jackson returned from the apartment and stood on the stoop with her.

The snow was really starting to come down now. Looking up at him, she smiled.

As he locked the door, she put her phone away and pulled her jacket tight around her. It was getting colder, but somehow, just looking at Jackson warmed her cheeks.

He reached out and took her hand. With the snow falling all around, he kneeled down on one knee.

"Emerson Nichols. Love of my life. Will you please spend the rest of your life with me?"

Emy shook in disbelief. She hoped this day would come. Making it official felt so good.

She wanted to remember this feeling and everything about this moment forever. She looked down at Jackson, still on one knee, and pressed her hand to her heart.

"I love you. Everything about you," he said, beeming.

He knew the answer to his question before he asked. He had wanted to propose to her a year ago, the minute they landed in New York on the way home from that first Christmas in Paris. It took everything in him to wait until this day.

Emy's hands flew up to her mouth.

"Yes! Yes, I'll spend the rest of my life with you!"

She pulled Jackson to his feet. He picked her up and swung her around.

"I love you, Emy. You make me a better person. I can't wait to live this life with you."

He kissed her before setting her back down on the ground.

"*Now* we're going to be late."

Emy heard someone yelling down the street as they approached the car. She knew the sound of that voice. She looked down the street and saw Chloe running toward them.

"Did she say yes? Did *you* say yes?"

Chloe ran down the block toward Emy. Patrick trailed behind, shaking his head at his crazy wife. Chloe waited impatiently around the corner before she sprinted toward Emy.

With tears in her eyes, Emy ran toward Chloe. The two collided in a hug and fell to the ground as they slipped in the wet snow.

"Of course, I said yes! And you knew this was going to happen?!"

Emy laughed and wiped her damp hair from her face.

"Of course I knew. Did you think I wouldn't know? I've known for months!"

"It's been killing me. This has been the hardest secret I've ever had to keep. When Jackson called me a few minutes ago, I told him to hurry up because I was already on my way over!"

Patrick walked past the two on the ground, knowing it was useless to try to help them up. They'd be there for a while. He reached out to shake Jackson's hand and congratulate him.

"Those two," Jackson said, laughing. "Always into something."

Patrick rocked back on his feet and watched them try to get themselves together.

"I wouldn't have it any other way."

Chloe got to her feet first and pulled up Emy with her.

After saying happy-tear goodbyes to Patrick and Chloe, Jackson and Emy finally hit the road to the Riley family gathering.

∞

"DOES YOUR FAMILY KNOW?"

Emy was still in awe of the ring Jackson had placed on her finger.

"They know I've wanted to marry you the second we touched down in New York a year ago, but they don't know I proposed today."

Jackson held her hand as they drove to Brooklyn.

When they pulled up to the house, she got out of the car and looked up at the beautiful brownstone. Jackson started pulling out the packages in the back. It wasn't long before the front door opened, and the chaos began.

Seeing them pull up, Jackson's nieces and nephews plowed down the stairs and up to the parked car. They were eager to see what was wrapped in the packages Jackson pulled out of the car.

Jackson loaded up the kids with bags, trying to get a word in as they begged to know what they had brought them.

Emy leaned back, chuckling to herself in disbelief. She savored the scene, as Jackson tried to hold his own but quickly became outnumbered.

"A little help here?" he said.

"No way. You're on your own."

She stood there laughing as Jackson tried to keep the kids from tackling him in the fresh snow.

Emy saw Jessica hurrying down the steps to greet them. She stopped and stood next to Emy. Instantly, Jessica could tell there was something different about her.

"Something's going on. Wait. Oh my gawd." Jessica looked back and forth between Emy and Jackson.

"Let me see your hand!"

Jessica let out a squeal, and the two women embraced. They stood on the sidewalk hugging as the rest of the family filed out of the house to see what all the commotion was about.

Jessica turned to the group and yelled, "He finally did it. He finally proposed to Emy!"

The entire family rushed down the stairs and then to the curb to congratulate them.

Jessica walked over to Jackson and gave him a hug.

"You did good, Jack."

There were tears in her eyes. Jackson and Jessica had a special bond, so he understood where the tears were coming from.

He slung his arm over her shoulder. They watched the family hover around Emy to get a look at her ring and welcome her to the family.

"I owe you one, sis. If it wasn't for you, I'm not sure we'd be here together right now."

As Jessica elbowed him in the ribs before walking away to join in the celebration, she reminded him…

"Don't you forget it."

Jackson's Running Playlist

Closer
The Chainsmokers, Halsey

Who
Jimin

Beautiful Things
Benson Boone

Houdini
Eminem

Remind Me to Forget
Kygo, Miguel

I Can Do It With a Broken Heart
Taylor Swift

Castle on the Hill
Ed Sheeran

Thunderstruck
AC/DC

Whatever
Kygo, Ava Max

Titanium
David Guetta, Sia

As It Was
Harry Styles

Lose Yourself
Eminem

Continue reading for a sneak peek of Chloe's
story in Camille's second book from the
Infinite Airlines series, *Cleared for Love*.

Cleared
FOR LOVE

CAMILLE HOPE

1

Chloe

WAS THAT COFFEE SHE SMELLED? Chloe rolled over and grabbed her phone to check the time.

Her parents started brewing coffee in the early morning hours to get Chloe up and moving. It had been three months since Chloe graduated from college. They were eager to see her do something with her life.

Chloe slipped her feet into her slippers and went downstairs to the kitchen.

"Morning!"

Chloe had always been a morning person—and apparently, a night person as of late. She walked across the kitchen and gave her mom a quick peck on the cheek.

"How's everyone today?"

Chloe moved over to the cupboard and pulled out a bowl. Cereal and milk were already on the table where her parents were seated.

"Things are good. Is there any word on the job front yet?"

Leave it to Chloe's dad to cut to the chase. She dumped Lucky Charms cereal into her bowl and poured milk over the top.

"Dad, you know what? You'll be the first to know."

Chloe had a huge smile on her face. Her parents couldn't resist her. They know she was a little too smart for her own good. It was because of her quick wit and sarcasm that may have prevented Chloe from landing a serious job.

Chloe knew she could irritate her dad easily. She loved her parents deeply as they did her, but she knew it was only a matter of time before they kicked her out.

They had put Chloe through college and allowed her the freedom she wanted. But now, they wanted her to start getting serious. Or at least a respectable job beyond working part time at the café down the street.

Living on Nob Hill in San Francisco, Chloe had access to some of the best restaurants, bars, and coffee shops. This allowed Chloe to bounce around from job to job until she could figure out what she really wanted to do.

Picking up her bowl, Chloe tilted it back and drank the remaining milk left over from her cereal.

"Really, Chloe? Have we taught you nothing?"

Chloe's mom came around the table and took the bowl from her daughter.

"You've taught me everything I know. You should be very proud."

Chloe could see her mom was starting to lose her patience. She got up and grabbed her favorite mug from the cupboard. *Probably Late For Something* was written on the mug in bold red type.

Chloe was always late. This was part of the reason she had yet to land a job. She had a hard time getting to her interviews on time.

Chloe sat back at the table with her coffee that had been decorated with too much cream and sugar. She took out her phone and started to scroll.

After a few minutes of silence at the table, Chloe slapped her hand down on the table, scaring everyone in the process.

"Hot damn, today is your lucky day, Dad!"

Chloe bolted up from the table and ran upstairs. Her mom looked over at her dad, who had been startled by his daughter's abrupt departure.

"What do you think that was about?"

"Who knows. Let's just hope she's right. Maybe today *will* be my lucky day," Chloe's dad said with a sigh.

Even though Chloe's parents wanted her to start thinking about her future, they loved having her around. It was her lifestyle they didn't approve of. Her parents loved their quiet life in the city, and Chloe was anything but quiet, making their retirement years unpredictable.

∞

CHLOE RAN UPSTAIRS AND HEADED TO HER CLOSET. Most of her clothes were in piles around the room. She was sure she'd find what she was looking for. She hadn't used it since her parents had gifted it to her during her senior year of college.

"Ahhh, here you are."

Chloe pulled out the traditional navy blue dress her parents had bought her and encouraged her to wear to job interviews. It still had the tags attached to it. Chloe walked over to the mirror on the back of the door and held the dress up to her.

"Wow, this is something."

Chloe turned around and tossed the dress on the bed before hopping in the shower. If she hurried, she could make it.

Stepping into the shower, Chloe thought about the last few months and how restless she had become. She had been so sure she would have landed her dream job by now. But Chloe didn't know what that job looked like.

She had moved back in with her parents hoping to figure out what she wanted to do. However, the last three months have proved more confusing than ever before.

Turning off the water, Chloe grabbed her towel and dried off. She did a quick mental checklist of what she needed to do and how fast she needed to get it done to be on time.

This would be the biggest challenge for Chloe yet, as she was always late. She prayed today would be the first step in turning her life around.

For updates and availability of this book and others by Camille Hope, visit *CamilleHope.com*.

Infinite Airlines

Buckle up and enjoy the ride with Emy, Chloe, Ava, Jessica, and more friends to come along the way. The women of *Infinite Airlines* are first class, and they each have a story to be told.

Acknowledgements

MY GRANDMOTHER, MAXINE. She believed I could do anything, even write. I wish I hadn't put down the pen so many years ago. She would have loved Emy and Jackson.

My incredible Beta Readers who were the first to get to know my characters and gave me such great feedback. Thank you Emelia, Ashleigh, Jessica, Mindy, Carrie, Emily, and Judie for the gift of your time. You'll never know how hard it was to hit send. But you were all so gracious and encouraging.

Thank you, Kate, for delivering the cover that lived only in my head. I didn't think it would be possible to make my imagination a reality. You have a gift.

My best friend and book club, Emelia. I am so thankful we share our love of books with each other. Thank you for listening to me ramble on endlessly each and every day.

Thank you to my biggest fan, my mother. I have heard you talk about my book to others, and I hear how proud you are when you do it. Thank you.

My husband. Without your love and support, this would never have come together. You even went as far as reading a romance novel or two to understand this genre. Not your cup of tea, but you did it anyway because you knew how much I wanted this to come together. And thank you for all your help getting this where it needed to be to become a reality. Your talents are endless and I really don't think you'll ever know how much I appreciate you.

I owe a lot of hugs and kisses to my girls. There were days where I was in a groove and couldn't be 100% present. I hope, one day, you follow your dreams and never let anything hold you back. And when you do, I will be your biggest cheerleader. I love you both so much.

To every ARC reviewer, Bookstagramer, and BookToker, thank you for tagging and engaging with me in your posts. It makes writing so much fun to know I've brought a little more joy of reading to you, and I'm grateful to you for helping promote my first novel.

And last but not least, my airline family. Especially my Delta girls. I have so many wonderful memories as a flight attendant, mostly because of getting to train and work with you. Even though many of us have our feet on the ground now, our friendships are still flying.

About the Author

CAMILLE HOPE is a contemporary romance writer who loves reading and writing feel-good books with predictable storylines. Feeling like life can be too heavy at times, she writes low-stress stories with happy endings and a dash of spice to keep them interesting. Pulling from past flight attendant experience, Camille writes fiction based on her time flying the friendly skies. For more information, please visit *CamilleHope.com*.

∞

Instagram: @camillehopeauthor
Threads: @camillehopeauthor